Your Secrets Sle

YOUR SECRETS SLEEP WITH ME

DARREN O'DONNELL

Coach House Books

Published with the assistance of the Canada Council for the Arts and the Ontario Arts Council. The publisher also acknowledges the assistance of the Government of Canada through the Book Publishing Industry Development Program and the Government of Canada through the Ontario Book Publishing Tax Credit Program.

NATIONAL LIBRARY OF CANADA
CATALOGUING IN PUBLICATION

O'Donnell, Darren, 1965-
           Your secrets sleep with me / Darren O'Donnell. – 1st ed.

ISBN 1-55245-138-0

           I. Title.

PS8579.D64Y68 2004   C813'.6   C2004-902056-0

' ... if we want to be equal to the absolutely new tasks ahead, we will have to abandon decidedly, without reservation, the fundamental concepts through which we have so far represented the subjects of the political (Man, the Citizen and its rights, but also the sovereign people, the worker, and so forth) and build our political philosophy anew starting from the one and only figure of the refugee.'

– Giorgio Agamben

0

1

2

3

4

5

6

7

8

9

10

You Don't

exist – for just this moment. So for just this moment there's nothing, nothing happening. For just this moment. Enjoy it because, sadly, it's gone.

You exist.

Now something is happening.

Let's say it's the radio. That much could easily be happening. Let's say it's the television. Or congested traffic. Let's say it's kids.

Here's a kid. And then over here, another kid, and over here another one. Let's say you're the sunshine bouncing into their homes, peeking into their windows and laying a little grace on them. There are kids everywhere. Here's one – a girl – she's sixteen. Here's a boy, he's thirteen. Here's an eight-year-old girl and an eleven-year-old boy. Here's another sixteen-year-old girl. They're all hanging out as you bounce in on them, shining bright as you are.

Say you were a kid. That could be happening. Try to imagine what that might be like. It's not like you've gotten where you are without having been one. If you have a second, make a list of all the things you've learned since then. Or forgotten since then. Which would be the bigger list?

Let's say it's the first day of summer. Look at the sky – the sun is hanging overhead taking its sweet time. The day is warm, bright and beautiful. And we hope we're not taking too many liberties when we say: so are you.

Over Here,

sixteen-year-old Kaliope Vally lies on a futon in the corner of a tiny room in a house somewhere downtown. She points a remote, her stereo the only thing she brought up from Dearborn, Michigan, just a couple of weeks ago. She's scanning the airwaves, trying to get a sense of this new city.

In addition to the stereo's remote she also holds her stomach. She's not feeling very well. The state of the world makes her nauseous.

'I can't stomach all the lies,' she's fond of saying. And it's true. She can't.

She decided to leave America a few days before the president declared Red Alert, before the streets started crawling with military, doors got busted down and people dragged away. She managed to get in by convincing the immigration official that she was just coming to visit the Hockey Hall of Fame.

Her real mission was – is – to find her legendary aunt, the long-lost Amina, a sister to her mother and famous in some circles. Someone in Detroit told Kaliope that her aunt had headed north a few weeks back. Or maybe it was a few months – time flies even when you're not having fun.

There's Also Another

someone, another kid, little eight-year-old Rani Vishnu. A nervous kid. Well, maybe not nervous but kind of an alert that might feel like nervous. And like nervous, it could get to be a little much. She had started going grey, a single strand standing out from shiny blackness.

And that was before the Red Alert.

Having been pinned down with her mother, Anu Vishnu, by a line of riot cops, engulfed in clouds of tear gas and shot at

with a couple of rubber bullets, the kid then sprouted a few
more.

Subsequently, when Anu witnessed a number of her
colleagues at the University of Michigan being rounded up
and detained, Rani had agreed that perhaps it was time to
follow some of her mom's research leads that pointed
north – until the dust settled.

Now they're stuck on the Queen Elizabeth Way, idling in
congested traffic, surrounded by construction and all the
other cars with American plates.

In the middle distance a yellow backhoe labours, tearing up
the road, vomiting exhaust into an already wheezing
atmosphere, and, way off, the CN Tower, world's tallest
freestanding structure, appears to be standing aloof. The
angle of the view creates the impression that it's edging
away from the rest of the city's buildings, contemplating
dipping its toes in the lake.

While over here there's another kid. Over here –

Here.

There's this kid. This kid in the bathroom. This white kid.
This really white kid. This sixteen-year-old named Ruth
Racco.

Ruth is locked in the bathroom staring at her face in the
mirror and ignoring her brother, Michael Racco, and
his friend James Hardcastle – that little piece of shit
who had walked on water – as they pound on the bathroom
door.

'I believe Ruth is staring at herself again,' Michael shouts to
the house.

Ruth remains fixated on her ghostly image.

Ruth had been born with vitiligo, a condition in which not only is there no melanin but there are no melanocytes, the cells that produce melanin. While she was gestating, her father, John Racco, backhoe operator, had punched Ruth's mother, Katherine, in the stomach. It was in play, he had claimed, and Katherine corroborated his story, stating that he had been pretending to be the great Muhammad Ali. Ruth was born premature and born white.

She's sixteen. She has spent the past year saving money and trying to convince her parents that she's old enough to move out; she needs to be downtown, because down there, there's a scene.

And This Is Her

brother, little eleven-year-old Michael, a kid with a few good food allergies. He's in his living room removing cushions from the sofa with his friend, the thirteen-year-old water-walker, James Hardcastle. James had walked on water in the fountain at the local mall in what was heralded as a miracle.

Back in the day, some thirteen years ago, James's mother, Joan Hardcastle, had simply decided to start dividing the egg herself. On a whim. To see if she could. And she could. Nine months later little James was born into obscurity. With no father, he had, at first, felt he was in some way deficient, not a whole boy. His walk across the water at the mall had changed all that. He was now a holy boy.

The state had taken a dim view of Joan Hardcastle, Jim's mother, hurling accusations of genetic manipulation and so forth, and, for the boy's own good, had sent little Jim to a group home.

When the miracle first occurred, James's name appeared in the newspapers on a daily basis. Over the course of the following months this gradually lessened and now it's hardly there at all. People still occasionally recognize him – like in the good old days – but even that's happening less and less. Soon the population of the city won't remember him at all.

And speaking of the city – it is, in fact, a teenage city, pubescent, a little nervous; masking shyness with a performance of aloofness; snooty but universally so and born only of an unawareness of just how beautiful it is. Still, efforts to distinguish oneself from forces that can be considered parental are reactionary and, ultimately, ugly. So, it's an ugly beautiful city; a shy city; a city that has a hard time saying hello to acquaintances. A sad city. A lonely city.

Kaliope Isn't Sure

what to make of the city. It sounds pretty ordinary on the radio. And if it's an ordinary city it shouldn't be that hard to find Amina. If her aunt has been here for more than a couple of weeks, people will know about her. She has a lot of charisma. She might be in a band. She always could rhyme. And talk. Amina could talk a lot too.

Kaliope rolls onto her stomach, stretching out, trying to relax. She lifts a *NOW* magazine – one of the city's eager entertainment weeklies – and opens it. The ads for the city's clubs fill a few pages, tight little ads with tight little text. Band after band after band. Kaliope clenches her jaw, shuts her eyes and holds down a burning in the middle of her chest. The sounds of the city's radio frequencies wash over her, a description of the city's busy traffic. Names new to Kaliope: the Don Valley Parkway, Yonge Street, Eglinton Avenue.

Kaliope speaks, testing the strange word: 'Eglinton.'

The radio tells her that the QEW is clogged with cars and construction.

Kaliope flips to the back of the *NOW* magazine.

Maybe she could take out a personal ad: 'niece seeks long-lost aunt.'

Back In Michael Racco's

living room, Michael and James are loading up their arms with sofa cushions. 'The only thing I can eat is the discarded water in which my mother boils the perogies,' jokes little eleven-year-old Michael. He doesn't feel particularly Ukrainian but his mother, Katherine, does and is mortified by the fact that she is, the sound of her voice wafting in from the kitchen. 'I know I'm not dumb. But what the hell, everyone occasionally fucks up.'

The swear causes both Michael and his taller friend, the thirteen-year-old James Hardcastle, to explode with laughter, run down the stairs, throw the cushions onto the roof of their fort and dive in.

'I'm going to fuck your mother,' says James.

'The fuck you are.'

'Some things are just meant to be.'

And speaking of Mrs. Racco, she is always making sure the scene is peanut free.

'A peanut-butter cookie? Please, put that away,' she says to Joan Hardcastle, James's mother, the two chatting over cups of coffee in the kitchen. 'A little oil from one peanut has enough power to flatten my kid fifty times over.'

The phone rings and Mrs. Racco grabs it, thinking it's her husband, John Racco, the backhoe operator, with the information that he'll soon be home with dinner: pizza from some pizza place, say, or Mexican fast-food style, or, ultimately, thick chicken. But it isn't John, it isn't her husband, it isn't a backhoe operator, it's that little kid – that little kid James, that kid who walked on water.

'Hello, Mrs. Racco.'

Mrs. Racco notices the call comes from the second line in the basement. 'Hello, James.'

'Hello, Katherine.'

'What can I do for you, James?'

'What can you do for me?'

'That's the question.'

'Well, you could swear in my ear.'

'I'm sorry?'

'Mrs. Racco, I have to tell you that I just feel like shitting my pants with desire.'

Mrs. Racco, surprised by the child's obscenity, knocks her knee into the table, the coffee cresting over the rim and into her lap.

'Fuck!' she exclaims.

And just at that moment laughter, 'hey,' and 'cut it out,' the phone banging and 'give it to me,' and more laughter, and finally Michael:

'Mom, be careful he wants to – '

Click.

Out On The

road, the situation on the QEW remains the same, with all cars stopped. Little eight-year-old Rani and her mom hang out playing games.

'Is it the sun?'

'Cold.'

'The banana.'

'Colder.'

'That flashing light.'

'Mommy, that's not yellow, it's orange.'

There's the sound of a dull explosion, a low crunching, crumpling metal and shattering glass.

'Is it that big machine?'

'Warmer.'

Anu continues looking at the big yellow backhoe, not understanding what she's seeing.

Back In The

cushion fort, James and Michael stare at the TV. A clip of the president talking about intelligence too sensitive to disclose, threats to the nation that are so serious that even to whisper them would jeopardize lives. There are images of tanks cruising America's streets, and long lines of cars broiling in the day's sunshine trying to get across the border. The anchor interrupts with breaking news: a high-angled shot of a highway, immobile traffic and a piece of heavy machinery. A big yellow backhoe, the shovel of which punches into cars, panicked people running for cover. The angle of the image shifts, revealing the backhoe operator in a close-up.

'Michael, is that your dad?'

'What?'

'It's your dad.'

The two boys stare silently at the television.

Little eleven-year-old Michael calls out. 'Mom! Dad's on TV!'

The Backhoe Is

roaring, its engine labouring, as John Racco manoeuvres the machine, punching the shovel through the roofs of car after car. From behind him, a man in a suit sprints up and clambers on board, reaches into his own pocket and removes a cellphone. His foot slips, and he nearly falls beneath the machine. Regaining his balance, he swings open the door of the cab and, using the cellphone as a weapon, administers a powerful blow to John Racco's temple. John collapses and the man in the suit lets John's inert body roll out of the cab and tumble to the ground. He then sits in the seat, examines the various levers, grips them and resumes what John Racco started: punching holes through the cars stuck on the Queen Elizabeth Way and the people in them.

A crowd has formed a safe distance from the spectacle. A helicopter descends, the red and blue logo of the Metropolitan Toronto Police prominent on its side. The chopper hovers low over the highway and an amplified voice commands the man on the backhoe, the details of the directive getting lost in the chopping din.

Little eight-year-old Rani Vishnu stands with the crowd, holding her mother's hand, and watches the police helicopter with curiosity. She has always been interested in power differentials. She had, in fact, recently come in second in the Science Fair with a model for an equitable, balanced and democratic conversation. 'You talk about you, I talk about you, I talk about me, you talk about me, you talk about you, I talk about you, I talk about me, you talk about me, and so on, until there's a good reason to stop.'

The project, simply entitled Fair Talk, was edged out of first place by a beautifully designed model, created by fifth grader Avril Anderson, that demonstrated the mechanics of evaporation and condensation.

'A cloud,' the little winner had stated, 'can be considered the soul of a lake.'

The helicopter dips in close to the backhoe. There's the sound of a couple of sharp cracks in quick succession and the glass in the front of the backhoe's cab shatters and blood and body matter splatter the back window.

Kaliope Stands In

her tiny room listening intently to the radio, the description of the action on the QEW coming in at real time from a news helicopter hovering somewhere. She looks out the window at the side of the neighbour's house, a crack of sky just visible, and scans fruitlessly for the helicopter. If there are maniacs, killing sprees and sharpshooters, it may not be such a bad town after all.

She had expected dog sleds.

The Evening News

has already given it a name – the Backhoe Massacre – and brought out a variety of experts on the phenomenon of unfettered rage, some applying the tenets of epidemiology and discussing a viral theory of emotional contiguousness. The second man involved – the man in the suit – has no connection to John Racco. He is a businessman named Daniel Young whose only resemblance to John is that they are both respected members of their communities, both fathers and little-league hockey coaches. The experts suggest that Daniel somehow contracted John's rage and that's why he did what he did. Why John did what he did, however, remains a mystery.

The news continues on Kaliope's stereo, the chatter shifting to the subject of refugees lining up to get across the border, people turned back, jailed, deported. Kaliope has heard that it isn't even only Muslims like herself anymore; poor neighbourhoods all over America are locked down, there are reports of people disappearing and security forces who don't bother to flash badges.

Kaliope's first serious encounter with the police was a few years back during a meeting of her father's community cricket team at a local church. A frightened neighbour, not used to seeing so many brown people in uniforms, dialed 911, resulting in the dispatch of the city's Anti-Terror Unit. No one was hurt, but the image of young – mostly white – men in military uniforms pointing an arsenal of deadly weapons at middle-aged brown men in cricket uniforms has become a permanent reference point in the kid's ideological canopy.

Kaliope lies on her bed listening for news about the conflict in America, about the massive protests in a couple of cities and about the car bomb that has been detonated outside a Homeland Security office. The American military, Kaliope's aunt Amina once claimed, has been training for years to deal with their own populations, practicing war manoeuvres in a variety of suburbs.

Sixteen-Year-Old

Ruth Racco chats to her little brother Michael, as he balances on the rocks outside the police station. 'How'd Dad look?'

'Focused.'

'I guess you won't have to play hockey this year.'

'No, I guess not.'

'Well that's a good thing.'

'True.'

'And I can move out now.'

'What am I supposed to do?'

'You'll be able to go soon.'

'Soon?'

'Well, in few years.'

Little Eight-Year-Old

Rani Vishnu's interest in the power differentials of policing was initiated by an incident in her very early years at a Gay Pride parade. A cop had slipped on a hot dog, which had been accidentally jostled out of someone's hand, and crashed down on top of the kid. Since then she has preferred to keep her distance from cops.

But now that's impossible – there are cops all around, shadows in the dusk, guarding the gates to the parking lot of a vast empty warehouse: Rani and Anu's new home. The warehouse is situated along the railway lines snaking up from the centre of the city, into the west end, then north and further west across the rest of the country. The building looks like it's been sitting quiet for a few years, not quite abandoned, just empty, waiting for some condensation in the evaporative process of the economic cycle, an upturn that many feel is coming. They always come.

Rani carries a couple of small bags and trails after Anu as they walk through the warehouse, passing people.

In a vast open area, a representative from the city explains that there are three dorm-like areas – one each for women, men and families. There's a common lounge area and a sort of kitchen for rudimentary food preparation, the bulk of the food being provided by the city in twice-daily deliveries. There are makeshift showers, and one of the phone companies has set up a trailer, providing pay phones to which phone cards are sold. The lights in the dorms are always kept on, in the day fully bright, in the night just slightly dimmed.

Rani stands, barely listening to the announcement, focusing her attention on the question of gravity. If the planet is spinning, why doesn't everyone just fly off? And if tossed off the globe, what then? Rani imagines a science project, herself onstage in the gymnasium with a piece of chalk in her hand.

'I envision floating communities,' she would say, 'with no ground, no permanent point of reference, and, with the universe always expanding, it would be impossible to agree to meet your friends. Nothing would ever be in the same place. Not even the same place. You'd have to be friends with whoever was there for however long they were there. The same would go for enemies.'

Ruth Racco Insists On

walking down from the suburbs along the railway tracks in the dark; she wants to feel the centre of the city leaking slowly into her body. James and Michael help carry some of her stuff. The sound of a helicopter chops high in the air, the CN Tower blinking in the distance.

'You make it sound as if not having a dad was somehow detrimental to you,' says Ruth.

'Well, it certainly didn't give me any advantages,' replies James.

Ruth rolls up her sleeves to reveal her skin, defenceless against the sun's rays. 'Yeah, well, you didn't get any disadvantages, either.'

'Whatever, your dad is a genius.'

Ruth grabs James by the front of the boy's T-shirt and slams him against a railway car.

'Our dad is a killer.'

'Look, sister, that dude had a point to make and he made it, so get your hands off me or I'll punch the colour back into you.'

'Suck me, you little fucker.'

'I was saving that for your – '

'Look.' Michael points toward one of many warehouses along the railway. In the parking lot there are cops, military and people pulling up in cars filled with possessions. It looks like families: some older people, some younger people and some kids. And stuff. Lots of stuff. The contents of their lives.

'They're American,' says Ruth.

'This city makes me puke.' James continues walking. 'They wouldn't recognize the miraculous if it grew hair on the streets.'

They reach the overpass where Dundas and College streets converge, the rich smell of the chocolate factory hovering in the air.

'Catch you later,' says Ruth as she makes her way up the embankment onto the streets, waves at her little brother, then disappears. In the southern distance, somewhere over the lake, there's a faint flash of lightning.

It's a dangerous city. There is one sewer somewhere downtown that is said to have eaten a child. The cops have a helicopter. People describe the inhabitants as 'cold.'
Like many in their teens, the city thinks a lot about suicide. But then, who doesn't?
It's an obvious one.
Like the nose on your face. Look at it – the nose on your face – you can see it as you read these words. It looks a bit abstract, floating out of focus, your eyeballs only catching fragments, blurred and inchoate but fully there. Just like suicide.

The City's Dusk

speeds along, propelled by the approaching storm, and infiltrates Kaliope's bedroom. She lets it slither in, choosing not to turn on the light. She sits in the room's only chair, leaning against an old kitchen table stuffed into a corner. The blue cast of her stereo illuminates the newspaper spread across the desk. She has settled on a station at the left-most reaches of the FM spectrum. Bhangra quietly leaks out of the speakers.
She studies the newspaper, taking particular interest in the section that focuses on the city, trying to learn more about her new locale.
The DJ on the radio lists the tracks just played. Outside, the rain begins to fall, spattering against the window. Kaliope reaches out and raises the volume. The DJ talks about the

recent deportation of an Algerian man who was dragged out of the sanctuary of a church. Kaliope turns up the volume. It's a very familiar voice.

And Here In The

hallway of his house there's little eleven-year-old Michael Racco peeking into his parents' bedroom and watching his sedated mother sleeping.

Michael clicks his mother's door shut, walks to his sister's old bedroom and enters without knocking. Ruth's collection of plush animals sits on a shelf, staring at Michael. Rain can be heard ticking the window. Michael stares at the toys and begins to speak to them.

'I once did a survey about suicide,' he says. 'Some people think Danes are most likely to kill themselves due to a pathological lack of sunlight, some people think the war-torn Sri Lankans, but, actually, most feel it's dentists.'

Michael allows a space for laughter.

'When I find my mind dwelling on the possibility of ending it all, I usually focus on one method, exploring all angles. These days I keep thinking about going to the tracks, laying my neck on the rails and shearing off my head. My only concern is that neural activity will continue long enough after the act to formulate anxiety or, worse, terror. I worry that final states of mind might be carried into the afterlife – eternal terror in heaven seems a more uncomfortable option than inert depression on earth. Don't you think?'

There's a rumble of thunder.

James Hardcastle,

tucked tight between the sheets of his bed at the group home, listens to the rain drumming on the roof. Turning his face skyward, he attempts to bask in the sunny benevolence of God.

'Am I getting a tan?' he asks his bunkmate, a young boy named Xiang Pao.

'No,' says Xiang.

'I'm telling you,' says young James, 'I can feel the presence of something.'

Shhh. Be very still.

And, Here,

Rani, eight years old and unable to sleep, stares at the ceiling of the vast warehouse, watching the rainwater begin to drip.

And Kaliope,

cramped in the corner of her room, wrapped in blankets, talking on the phone with her aunt, the rain outside, feeling like it is washing relief into her body.

And Then Ruth,

standing downtown at the intersection of Yonge and Dundas in the middle of the square in the middle of a rainstorm, illumination provided by all the televisions beaming their advertising into the faces of the multitudes.

Then lightning flashes, followed by a quick clap of thunder, people hearing it at different times.

And Then ...

What happens next will be the source for many discussions about the state of the world, the nation, the city, the environment and the populace.

The dark purple clouds begin twisting and touching down, a tornado forms, thundering and careening into the city, knocking over its point of pride: the world's tallest freestanding structure, the CN Tower, lifting it and dropping it right into the lake.

0

1

2

3

4

5

6

7

8

9

10

As The Structure Formerly Known As

the world's tallest freestanding lies in the lake waiting for news of a better day, there's heated talk among the other buildings, a debate that rages around whether the tower can't get up or won't get up. The smaller, older buildings all seem to agree that it can but won't, while some of the bigger bank buildings claim that won't is the same as can't, that a loss of will is a loss of will and once the juice is gone the juice is gone, you might as well use the thing as the first leg in a walkway connecting to America.

Little eleven-year-old Michael Racco is concerned that the toppled tower is his fault, a response to an idea he is unaware he had thought. He sits in the dark basement talking on the phone to his sister, Ruth, who lies on the floor of her bedroom, fresh in her new place on Euclid Avenue, down in the heart of the town. Outside, the rain continues, the second day in a row.

'Dad is evil,' says Michael.

'My skin bears witness to the effects of Dad, so don't talk to me about evil.'

'Ruth, you've got to get me out of here.' Michael grips the phone, his knuckles turning white. 'I'm fifty pounds heavier when I'm in this house; I can't breathe.'

Ruth herself is cramped with eight roommates: some students, some seniors, and some kid across the hall who moved in not too long before Ruth.

'Just be patient. Before you know it you'll be old enough to do whatever you want.'

'I didn't know the dead can do whatever they want.'

'Don't be so dramatic.'

'Ruth, the air in here is too thin to sustain life.'

'Look, Michael, I've got to get to yoga.'

'Ruth, do the evil know they're evil?'

A small murmur of thunder rumbles in from a distance.

Are you evil? A little?

Shaking The Gates

of the city is the horrifying case of the couple who kept their
two children in large glass jars, holes punched in the lids
for air.

That isn't all. There's also shit floating in the lake; kids pushing through loose screens to tumble out of high-rise apartments; the leader of the police union enjoying the post-
operative benefits of a pig's penis surgically grafted to his
own; and the maintenance crew at the National Hockey
Arena, a bunch of guys who fucked little fans for years.

Little eleven-year-old Michael Racco tries his best to view his
tendency toward an all-pervasive sense of loneliness as a
force that drives him headlong into an ever-widening expe-
riential expanse. His view of this feeling as a tendency
rather than a response is a deliberate tactic, an attempt to
encompass the desolation within a volitional circle: a
framework of intention.

'I want to be lonely,' he insists to the dormant television.

Seeking debate, he remotely activates the device to find
himself face to bow with an animated image of a seafaring
vessel and the accompanying narration, which states, 'The
sailors of yesteryear used the stars as a guide and regarded
them as their best friends.'

It's at this moment that Michael crystallizes his view of isolation, coining a phrase he will repeat over the course of a number of his life's phases: 'My friendships, like the constellations of antiquity, serve as my life's compass, while my loneliness will always be the wind within my sails.'

Michael maintains that if he eventually gets around to killing himself, the choice to die must be grounded in what he, and only he, thinks, feels, thinks he feels and feels he thinks. Suicide, he maintains, must be a solo show, performed, or not performed, for no one but yourself.

In That Warehouse

along the tracks is that other kid, that little eight-year-old kid with a few grey hairs – one more now since witnessing the Backhoe Massacre – that Rani Vishnu kid, sitting surrounded by a bustle of adults improvising buckets to catch the water from the leaking roof. A drop lands on the crown of Rani's head. Lightning illuminates the room through opaque windows high in the ceiling, and the children, gathered in a circle, begin to count.

'One Mississippi, two Mississippi, three Mississi – '

The thunder claps, and the kids scream.

That same thunder has, a few seconds earlier and a few miles away, sounded concurrent with the lightning that strikes a nearby tree as Michael Racco joins James Hardcastle on the porch of James's group home. Sheets of rain obscure the view of the dark street.

The boys discuss the climate, linking weather patterns to patterns of disease. There have been a number of medical problems to hit the city recently: meningitis, bacteria, atypical pneumonia, tuberculosis, viruses of all sorts, air unfit to breathe, water unfit to drink – it's stressful.

Little eleven-year-old Michael Racco wonders if it's possible to view the proliferation of pedophiles similarly – a problem with the environment, with the weather.

'But, frankly, they actually appear to be completely typical; most seem like regular guys to me,' he says to James, who gazes into the rain. 'Nothing really anomalous about them. They dress normally and wear their hair in typical styles.'

'Do you view that as good or bad?'

'Well – '

'Because, let me tell you,' James raises his voice against a swell of distant thunder, 'I need some sort of identifying trait – I've got to know from whom exactly not to accept a lollipop. I mean, I love lollipops.'

Sixteen-Year-Old

Kaliope Vally, the kid just up from America, is in the bathroom of her new place on Euclid Avenue, vomiting thin yellow strings of bile, having spent the day throwing a Frisbee against the impenetrable glass of the bank buildings on Bay Street.

Sixteen-year-old Ruth Racco knocks on the door. 'I've got to get to my yoga class. Can't you get a bucket or something?'

Kaliope speaks into the toilet. 'Why don't you try doing yoga in a bucket?'

'Why are you always puking?' Ruth asks through the door.

Ruth maintains that the world is an uneasy gathering of idiots and that suddenly something will blow and everything will be either okay or not okay.

Kaliope is always amazed at what those folks with white skin don't know. 'What you gain in privilege,' she often says, 'you lose in knowledge.'

Ruth speaks of a yearning for a dope spot spinning, the hole in the centre of the record, a place reserved for her.

The centre, Kaliope knows, extracts blood from the periphery to make up for the lost knowledge traded for the gained privilege.

Kaliope pukes again, the pit of her stomach squeezing her pubic bone out of her mouth. Ruth hops up and down, the need to pee unbearable. The rain buffets the house and a flash of lightning leaves behind an explosion that feels like it happened exactly between Kaliope and Ruth, two girls who generally walk around with a sense of impending doom, different for each, but similarly hollowing – if you listen carefully at their chests you can sometimes hear strands snapping like the pulled innards of a pumpkin.

Five seconds later the thunder is heard at the warehouse, and the circle of children screams with delight.

Ten seconds later the thunder is a distant rumble on the porch of James's group home.

Fourteen-year-old Xiang Pao steps onto the porch and offers James and Michael some candy.

'Michael, this is Xiang. He's a communist.'

'Hey, Xiang, thanks for sharing your candy.'

'My pleasure.'

Sheets of rain obscure the dark street.

'Michael's a little concerned he's radically evil.'

Michael shrugs and smiles. 'Well, my father is.'

James frowns. 'Your father is just inarticulate.'

Xiang sits beside James on the ragged couch and stretches his long legs. 'I've seen evil.'

'I wonder,' says Michael, 'if we might one day isolate an evil gene in the DNA of pedophiles.'

Xiang shrugs. 'I've always wanted to have sex with an adult, why not they with me?'

'An abuse of power,' says Michael, 'is always evil.'

'And is evil always an abuse of power?'

'Of course.'

Xiang shivers and retracts his legs, lifting his feet onto the sofa. He hugs his knees and gazes off into the rain. 'As I lie in bed at night, I find that in the state between awake and asleep I can become a hydrogen atom bound to two oxygen atoms. Before I drop off entirely, I'm able to travel through a couple of cycles from puddle to steam to cloud to rain and back to puddle again. My sense of myself as evil or good seems to pass through a similar process.'

A trickle of sweat rolls down Xiang's face.

'Are you okay?'

'I don't think so.'

Xiang had been shipped from China to Vancouver with a bunch of other youths, all sewn into plush toys, Xiang himself encased in Mickey Mouse. Six of the boys had died of dehydration. Xiang had been apprehended when he was discovered clinging, half frozen, to the underside of a truck bound for America.

'I should lie down.'

'I think I might be in love with that guy,' says James, after Xiang has gone.

In The Warehouse,

Rani walks down the dusty hall, away from the other kids, past a dank washroom and down some concrete stairs. A tall white man in a uniform stands smoking near the door.

'You can't go out, it's raining.'

'I just want to look at it.'

The man shrugs. Rani opens the door. Rain is falling; the tracks can barely be seen as hard sheets of water slide off the building and drop to the ground.

A tiny trickle tickles the door frame and a small puddle gathers at Rani's feet.

'Shut the door, you're flooding the fucking place.'

Rani shuts the door.

Back At The

house on Euclid Avenue, Ruth has left a small puddle of urine in front of the bathroom door. After Kaliope steps in the puddle, she leaves a small round patch of vomit in front of Ruth's bedroom door.

The house doesn't comment, attempting to remain as objective as possible by pretending it doesn't exist. Or that it's a cloud. And that this is heaven. And somewhere there's God. But the doorbell is broken. So you've got to keep knocking.

Little Eleven-Year-Old

Michael Racco views God as his equal – not someone who you'd expect to leave you outside in the rain but someone who would invite you in for coffee. Or, sometimes he doesn't believe in God at all but instead views the presence that he often thinks he feels as merely aspects of himself of which he is unaware. He doesn't worry about doing evil, he worries about being evil. But the possibility of working in league with the forces of darkness doesn't provide him with security, or power, or satisfaction; he doesn't plan to kill any kids at school. He doesn't he even like the kids at school, why would he do them any favours?

'If they want to die, they can do it themselves.' He speaks aloud in the dark, unable to sleep. Rocking himself to sleep with images of destruction just isn't working.

He steps out, pyjama clad, into the warm night. The thunderstorm, only just finished, has left behind a thick haze, heavy like a blanket from the old country.

Which old country? Any old country.

Little Eight-Year-Old

Rani Vishnu wakes from a dream in which a man speaks intimately with her, his mouth filled with buzzing flies. The large, hard, hollow room in which Rani lies echoes with coughs, the dim light keeping many from anything but just scratching sleep. There are some people sitting, some talking quietly, a faint murmur of music coming from headphones and a baby's fitful cries.

Rani slips her shoes on, walks down the dank hall past the dirty washrooms, turns a corner, ducks down the dusty stairs, tiptoes past the snoring security guard, then out of the tired warehouse and into a night warm and thick from the day's downpour.

Fourteen-Year-Old

Xiang Pao lies shivering in the arms of his roommate, James, and whispers into the boy's ear.

'I'm feeling more and more like steam.'

'You feel solid to me.'

Xiang coughs. 'I'm glad to be alive – '

The two boys kiss.

'– and in America.'

'You're not in America.'

'I'm sorry, of course not.'

Rani Gazes Across

the railway tracks that zip their way south toward the city's centre, and, north, through the suburbs and across the country. Elaborate graffiti decorates concrete walls, intricate tags and designs, the largest of which can be faintly discerned by the light of the night's moon. It says: 'You can hide your unexamined beliefs from yourself but your actions, even those as insignificant as the movement of an eyeball, will always give you away.'

'Hi.'

Rani Vishnu's eyes shift off the wall and down to the middle of the tracks, her pupils expanding in the dark. Little eleven-year-old Michael Racco stands there, his shape vague.

'Hi.'

'How old are you?' he says.

'How old are you?' she says.

'How old do I look?'

'Eight.'

'I'm small for my age.'

'Eighteen?'

'I'm eleven, my name is Michael, I live over there. I couldn't sleep.'

It's Dark In

the house on Euclid Avenue, and most of the occupants are sleeping, as a helicopter makes its lazy way over the city.

The night could be called beautiful, with a warm and rich humidity, the finest of haze which, if examined closely, is composed of an infinite mist, each microscopic droplet of water containing tiny misanthropic microbes. To be truthful, the air is alive with hate.

Toward you humans, that is.

Or, no, not hate but hunger. It wants to eat you.

Now, you'd best keep your immunity in order or you might be dinner. Or dessert.

A thin chocolate bar slices across the floor, traversing the crack of light that illuminates the small space beneath the door, coming to a halt in the centre of sixteen-year-old Kaliope Vally's bedroom. Kaliope – lost in the text of Franz Fanon's *Wretched of the Earth* – looks up to locate the source of the sound. The chocolate bar is still. A quiet voice, muffled by the door, speaks on behalf of the candy. Or maybe it's the other way around. In any case, someone says:

'I think we got off to a bad start.'

The tiny airborne microbes back off.

Conciliation, you might say, is good for the body.

'A Couple Of Years

ago a fox chased me down these tracks,' says little Michael Racco as he walks beside little Rani Vishnu.

'These tracks are some of capitalism's main arteries.'

'And to think, here we are walking on them.'

'Yes.'

'What, then, would be capitalism's heart?'

'The workers.'

'Of course. And the brain?'

Rani looks east at the buildings that glitter in the distant downtown. 'There.'

'A brain certainly can't live without a heart.'

'Not that I know of.'

'I didn't get your name.'

'Rani Vishnu.'

'Michael Racco. Vishnu – ?'

The two kids shake hands.

'Isn't that a god?'

'It is.'

The kids walk in silence.

'But – can a heart live without a brain?'

'Actually,' says Rani, 'a heart can keep on pumping even when the brain can't generate enough juice to formulate the urge to invest in an income trust.'

Michael nods. 'I read that radiation from cellphones causes accelerated growth in the area of the brain responsible for the sense of humour.'

'Really?'

'The afflicted seem to be able to understand jokes that absolutely no one else can.'

Back At The

house on Euclid Avenue, Kaliope and Ruth lie curled on the futon, their breath warm with chocolate.

Kaliope draws a strand of her own hair out of her mouth and speaks: 'I can't have sex with someone without feeling something.'

'Yeah, I usually feel dread.'

'Mixed with ennui?'

'Is that what that feeling is?'

'I usually feel nausea.'

Sixteen-year-old Kaliope Vally's grandparents are from Algeria; some of her grandparents' parents had come from Kenya, Tunisia and, before that, India, while some other grandparent's grandparents had come from France.

Ruth, on the other hand, insists that she is descended from Hannibal's army.

'So, technically, as a Carthaginian,' she says to Kaliope, 'I could be related to you.'

Ruth has one vivid memory of a great-grandmother who had lined up all the cousins, some as young as four, taken them one by one onto her lap and forced them to shoot an ounce of peppermint schnapps. There had been a slight sense that something perverted was happening.

'It *was* technically illegal,' says Ruth.

'Please.'

'Something imported from the old country.'

'Uh huh.'

'You know?'

Hope and despair need to be kept in careful balance. They are the two poles that alternate and maintain the charge that makes sure the motor runs.

Or so Kaliope says. In times like these, you're dead if one side of the equation malfunctions and ceases. Hope, without its sad counterpart, can lead only to an occluded view that fails to take into account all the horrors, while despair leads, as everyone knows, to death.

The image of her father and his cricket team pinned down by the emergency task force can jump out at Kaliope at any moment. And does.

'Is it worse,' she wonders aloud, 'to be the dead or the living dead?

'Even if that death is by suicide in some lonely woods?' Ruth asks.

'It's all about balance. The world between hope and despair is as close to life as anyone is able to muster, and it requires a patience bordering on boredom.'

'In times like these,' says Ruth.

'Yes,' says Kali. 'In times like these.'

A moment passes.

Their mouths move in.

Their lips don't touch.

Just.

One of the girls breathes in. The other breathes out. The air moves back and forth, never leaving the orbit of their bodies, the same lungful, circulating for what might well be hours.

Days.

Could've happened over the course of a light year.

A light year?

No, not a light year – a light year is a measure of *space*, not time.

In any case, they breathe together. Their lips not touching.

Just.

That Night, James

awakes with a start. A translucent version of Xiang stands at the foot of his bed, panic gripping the boy's face.

'Jim, you've got to help me!'

Xiang explains that as he was falling asleep he transmigrated into water and began to let his body cycle through the evaporative process.

'It was just a game. I play it every night. But I always come back,' he insists, tears rolling down his cheeks, hiccups jarring his story.

During his trip through the cycle, he drifted, in cloud form, too far north and fell as snow. He was squeezed by the weight of a deep drift, was compressed into water, then leaked down into the earth, coming, finally, to rest in the permafrost of Nunavut, a glacial Arctic bedrock, frozen forever.

'I'm trapped, you've got to help me!' he pleads before dissipating into thin air.

And Then Someone Has

a dream. It features a mollusc-like creature – two organisms, in fact, symbiotically intertwined. One, a gelatinous entity capable of accumulating the vibrations generated by sound and converting them into matter, and the other, a shell-like being that surrounds the jelly and functions as an exoskeleton. This latter creature lives only through the efforts of the former, not possessing the ability to collect food or synthesize its own nutrients, instead exacting nourishment from the jelly through a filimental root system.

The exterior appearance of the shell-like organism is ornate and colourful, with complicated patterns of bumps, grooves and intricately detailed markings, all serving no practical purpose and all at the expense of the jelly-like animal. The shell, in turn, provides a form, keeping the jelly within rigid confines, maintaining cohesion and preventing thirsty animals from sucking the jelly out of existence.

'It's win-win,' the shell is fond of saying. The jelly, however, has begun to question the benefits, and wonders just exactly how freedom would feel. Elements within the jelly argue that, without the shell, anarchy would ensue, they would fall apart, dispatched and dissolved into the unforgiving ground, while others talk of the jelly's inherent resilience, citing historical evidence supporting a shell-less past. The shell reacts to the debate with frightened brutality, sucking more nutrients than ever and creating a thicker shell with ever more intricate designs, structures that protrude castle-like, as if the threat to its existence comes from without and not, horrifyingly, from within its very core.

Soon, sound – the very source of its nutrition – begins to experience difficulties reaching the jelly.

In the dream, the dreamer dreams of lifting the creature, placing it in the mouth and cracking it with the teeth, the jelly sliding down the throat, somewhere between an oyster and an egg yolk, the little dude settling in the stomach to live forever on the sounds of a gurgling tummy, a tummy hungry for something. The shell, on the other hand, is simply composted.

In The Morning,

Xiang is gone, the coordinator of the home claiming that, in the night, the boy fell gravely ill.

'While I, Myself,

can merely walk on water,' Jimbo solemnly explains to Michael over a cappuccino, 'this beautiful boy, Xiang, *is* water.'

'Ice,' Michael corrects.

'Well,' says James, 'anyone can walk on ice, but this dude – '

Michael finishes the sentence. ' – *is* ice.'

James looks his younger friend dead in the eye.

'I've got to find him. And I've got to melt him.'

There Are A Lot

of kids holed up in the warehouse, but little eight-year-old Rani Vishnu doesn't feel she has much in common with them. Or whatever, she does, but with all that in common it's like getting to know yourself.

'Why do I need to get to know myself?' Rani asks her mother, who places a bowl of vegetable soup in front of the kid. 'I am myself.'

Anu touches Rani's head. 'Is that another grey hair?'

The kitchen area has been hastily created only for washing dishes and slicing fruit, the bulk of the food being distributed from trucks that arrive twice daily. The city keeps an alert eye on the situation, squeezed by the concern of nearby homeowners that the refugees may be carrying disease. There are fears that stray bits of food will attract vermin, the weather having been blamed already for a bump in the rat population. External food is forbidden.

The residents of the warehouse have already started talking about a legal challenge, while the mayor has pointed out that things can't be expected to run as smoothly as during peacetime, later apologizing, saying he didn't intend to imply the country was at war.

Little eight-year-old Rani swallows a soggy noodle. 'This is the kind of food they feed to the homeless.'

Anu removes the bowl from the table. 'Rani, we are the homeless.'

Rani Runs Down

the gloomy corridors of her building, past sealed units, empty probably. She runs past graffiti slashed into the walls, exposed wires and ducts overhead. She runs through dark sections, the buzzing tubes overhead offering only occasional illumination. She runs into the bowels of the building, the darkness engulfing her. The temperature seems to rise, the beautiful smell of the rotting building thickening. She stumbles upon a bunch of kids sitting quietly in the warm semi-darkness.

A little girl speaks. 'There is a certain sad something that corners me into a position where the only people to whom I feel romantically inclined are those not of my own race.'

'Yes,' chimes in Rani. 'The most astonishing achievement of the current economic arrangement is the near universalization of self-hatred.'

The little girl looks at Rani. 'You have a grey hair.'

'I have five.'

An older girl speaks. 'Self-hatred is a pattern of energetic excess, like bruised flesh. The way through the impasse is to find a way to redistribute the force. Look at this bruise.' She pushes up her sleeve to reveal a purple stain, someone's grip having ruptured cells. 'Now watch.'

All the children gather to observe.

The older girl pulls a little boy toward her and punches him on the shoulder. He screams. The other kids monitor the effect.

'He's bruising,' they agree.

'Now look at mine.'

The kids watch. And wait.

Leaving The Small

gathering of kids behind, Rani walks alone down the warehouse's dark, cool hallway. Off in the corner a few pieces of dried cat shit sit greying, turning to powder, and in the air is a strange smell. It seems to be emanating from the floor, perhaps the very soul of the building. Rani kneels down and lowers her nose, the building smelling like it has been infiltrated with mould, fungus, microbes – in its decay, more alive than ever, its entire body a flourishing ecosystem. It feels good. To both itself and to Rani.

A woman carrying a heavy bag walks down the hall.

'Do you want to help me take some dirt to the roof?'

The Rooftop Garden

is corralled with planks and cinderblocks. Rani digs holes for pumpkin seeds. The sun is bright and the earth smells rich. Peas are planted, and squash, potatoes, cabbage, carrots, tomatoes, basil, green onions and parsley.

There's a commotion below: the sounds of loud voices, laughter, a little applause and some cheers. Rani runs to the edge of the roof.

Two stoves and a fridge, purchased with pooled resources, are carried into the building.

In The Middle Of

the Eaton Centre is a massive stone bowl rimmed with a thin pipe that gently squirts arcs of water up and into the middle until the bowl is entirely filled. There's a pause, the bowl drains, the weight of the disappearing water dragging the attention of the shoppers along with it, making way for a thumping and three jets shooting straight up past three levels of shopping. The water hesitates near the arched glass ceiling then plunges down again to be caught, gathered and drained away, the bowl falling silent for a moment before the cycle resumes.

These three sudden jets of water cause children to scream with uncontrolled delight. Most kids yearn to be tossed into the air – that much is certain – and great heights are clearly possible.

James walks through the mall looking at all the beautiful people and contemplating his future. He circles the fountain, watching the geyser shoot up into the building's stratosphere. He feels he could be central to catalyzing some great movement; he just needs a scheme to recapture the love and attention of the populace. He feels anyone could be this, do this – it's just a matter of right time, right place, right attitude.

As he walks past People's Jewellers, a number of diamonds catch the light and toss glints into his eyes. A little boy, maybe five years old, steps in front of James, looking like a miniature version of Xiang Pao. The little kid flexes the tiny muscles of his arms at James.

The mall is a big, legendary place – famous worldwide. A complete ecosystem, a miniature city, a groundbreaking design, but still, it, too, is just holding it together, needing to focus all its energy on simply keeping up with the times, intertwined as it is with a struggling national identity.

James loves malls. It is no accident that his walk across water happened in one. He finds malls sexy; they give him energy. Looking at the multitude in malls is like observing them in their pyjamas – radiating a soft and warm vulnerability, naked almost. No, not almost – in some ways they are actually naked, the yearnings glittering in their eyes a form of tumescence. Everybody walks around malls in an inflamed state, and the mall collects and concentrates it, offering some suggestion of community, comfort, warmth, security and an easy understanding of the world.

The mall is just a conversation, an exchange of energies. The desire to interlock and transmit energy is a desire as old as DNA: people want to smash themselves together, rub property, give a little, take a little – it's natural. The mall is a beautiful place. It fills young James, fills him up.

With the future.

He stares at a flock of geese, a famous sculpture by a famous artist in that famous mall in that famous city, a city that worries it hasn't lived enough.

The city is looking for a bit more life experience; it feels, perhaps, that there is something of historical significance that hasn't yet happened and, until it does, there will be minimal movement.

Yet it's a city filled to the brim with its own power – it just isn't sure how to exercise it.

James regards the geese, an entire flock, life-sized replicas dangling from the ceiling on wires, caught in the penultimate moment of landing, the lead goose eternally spreading its webbed feet in anticipation of contact; the rest of the team securely behind him, all systems go.

Air! He can just up the stakes and walk on *air!* Walking on air would get him the kind of fame that would be discussed long after his death. And, further, because it's a skill he can share, teaching the multitudes the secret to the skies, it could last forever! He will do this for the people. And the people will repay him with fame; he will convert the fame to cash, the cash will buy a ticket to Nunavut and, once in Nunavut, he will free Xiang from the ice.

And, aside from all those obvious benefits, walking on air will allow him an existence that doesn't require contact with anything but air. And air, James maintains, makes very few demands. Except, of course, as wind. But as long as direction makes little difference, the exquisite trick is simply to go where the wind blows. Match your desire to the desire of the elements and you'll all get along just fine.

Kaliope Hangs Out,

leaning against the railing on the back porch of her aunt's place.

The coffee pushes in all the usual directions – it pushes against the present, past and future, connecting them to pure potential; it pushes against all the many things that can go wrong; and it pushes against Kaliope's sense of self, helping to stretch and spread its tendrils.

Kaliope searches for the place where she leaves off and everything else begins.

She can't find it. Maybe it's not there.

Look at your thumb. Is it attached to anything?

Where do you leave off? Where does your world begin?

Look for thin filaments that web your thumb off into everything. Are they there? Either you see them or you don't.

Or you see them more or less clearly.

And if you see them too clearly you can become paralyzed; it will look like there's nothing but a web – you're nothing but a web. So some say.

And those same some say, so as not to panic, it's best to keep your eyes half open, blur the world. And if that starts to look like a web then open your eyes really, really wide.

Then close them again. Alternate. Find a pattern. Look for a groove.

Amina sits on a stump of wood, a chunk of tree trunk upon which, in black magic marker, is written 'The Refugee Backlog.'

She's an MC, a thinker, an owner of a massive collection of books and the host of a radio show on one of the campus stations, a station still able to stand by the word 'revolution' – a courageous radio station ... or delusional. Or hopeful. Or prescient. Or all of the above. Her show, *You, Me and the Bourgeoisie*, features tunes, commentary and analyses of the situation.

She's a bit of a superstar in some circles, known to break the hearts of both the ladies and the men, but her biggest claim to fame, by far, is the line she has on a wicked bean. She has managed to gain access to a quality of coffee unheard of by the rest of the populace – coffee said to be the finest, having been spirited away by the workers, one bean at a time, and which, legend goes, is never sold but, instead, shared only with friends and family. To taste this coffee, some say, is to taste freedom.

'A person is sick ... ' Amina speaks over her steaming espresso.

'Yes?' says Kaliope.

'And they are given medicine that makes them feel more sick ... '

'Yes?'

'When they are eventually able to refuse the medicine, what will happen?'

Kaliope doesn't hesitate. 'They will feel better. But – '

'Yes?'

' – the person shouldn't confuse this improvement with wellness.'

Amina nods and sips her coffee. The morning is hazy, humid and hot, the air thick with pathogens, the young, the old and those with respiratory conditions having been cautioned to remain indoors.

'You want to know about this country?' Amina rhetorically asks. 'Well, what it looks like to me is a post-conquest capitalist state, economically wed to the U.S. – and that's spelled M-A-R-R-I-E-D – and inextricably tangled in English and U.S. imperialist projects, with aspirations of its own. It's an ideological fabrication, sublimating violent acts of theft and instituting them into formal stabilization, as tenuous as that stability might be.'

'Yeah, sure,' Kaliope says. 'But everybody knows that.'

Amina takes a sip of her coffee. 'How are you defining "everybody"?'

'Well, like, most of the world.'

'Oh, yeah, well, then sure, sure, everybody does knows it.'

'Have you ever noticed,' Kaliope says, 'that applying the languages of both of the country's conquering peoples, the word "mortgage" can be translated as "gauge of death"?'

'That's good. Mind if I use that?'

'If you give me a cut.'

'How about another coffee?'

'By the way, where do you get this stuff?'

'That's a long story.'

The back porch drifts in time, the coffee keeping minds alert and focused on the lazy swirls and counterswirls of the smoke from Amina's cigarette.

As an early expatriate from America, Amina is a student of freedom and the fights and flights that it necessitates. She slips Kaliope books about revolutionary headspaces and movements, state-sponsored terror, the nation's vertically arranged mosaic; books about meetings in barns between sovereigntists and the black revolutionaries of long ago; books about beatings, burnings and wiretaps, about communities intentionally flooded with drugs.

The two discuss politics: the injured, the angry, the tortured and the thoroughly bled; the recent half-millennium and the lost and the obscured, everything escalating, squeezed and wrought from the bones of billions. The colonial road trip stretching from pre to post to neo, locations along the way mentioned, pockets of resistance here and everywhere – the Black Panthers, Tamil Tigers, Tupak Amaru, the Sandanistas, the Zapatistas, the Shining Path, the FLQ, the IRA, PLO, the Shushwap Nation – individuals caught in the same line of fire that stretches from the streets of that supremely sickening city to an ever-widening circle of atomization.

They laugh about letters to the editors of local papers, assertions that the American refugees shelter undesirable elements who plan to foment terror, their intentions, some say, almost as visible as skin.

They talk of recent advancements in surveillance technology, dwelling on, in particular, a new device to hit the scene – Rage Radar or, more commonly, Racco Radar, after John Racco, author of the Backhoe Massacre.

Racco Radar is able to scan individuals and detect energetic patterns indicating emotional stress, excitement and anger. Airports and main thoroughfares are being equipped in order to scour the populace for anyone who might be feeling a little out of sorts. These people are then flagged, detained and interrogated.

The whole thing is causing consternation as people are pulled aside and subjected to rigorous psychological examinations and background searches which delve into, among other things, charities donated to, organizations belonged to/worked for, letters written to newspapers and recent purchases made with credit cards.

'They stop us for simply being black, and when this upsets us, they pick us up again,' says Amina, emphasizing the point with a stab of her cigarette.

And it's true – black and brown people, frustrated from being arbitrarily stopped by the cops, are being subsequently stopped again, deemed too angry for the good of society and sent packing to countries they haven't seen since they were two years old.

It is becoming very dangerous for some people to be anything but happy.

Kaliope Rides Her

bike down Spadina Avenue, away from her aunt's apartment, around 1 Spadina, home of the eyeball bank, and across College. She feels a flutter in her chest. It can push laughter up to catch in her throat, sometimes even threatening to tumble out of her eyes.

She looks at the people on the sidewalks, the inhabitants of that sexy city, sexy people in and of themselves, beautiful, not-quite-famous people, excellent people, shy people.

The population could use a big hug, that much is true.

Then again, who couldn't?

Kaliope expands in all directions, slicing her way down the street, clicking into all the streetcar tracks she traverses.

If you lay your ear on the tracks you can tune into many of the different conversations that are happening on the various streetcars, the talk reverberating down into the seats, into the wheels, then shaved and sent spinning into the tracks which zip them back, forth, up and down the city's streets.

The loudest of the conversations manage to reverberate themselves further, up from the rails into the wheels of other vehicles, further, even, into the bodies of the passengers; Kaliope notices a small tingle in her hands as she coasts her bike south down Spadina Avenue across the tracks on College Street.

The conversations are mostly ordinary – work, groceries and other responsibilities. A lot of them feature people busy putting each other in their place.

The rails take the conversations, sort them and shake out a sense of always doing, doing, doing. A little boy had once been lulled to sleep by the bustle, his tiny ear pressed to the rail, a contented smile secure on his face, when a streetcar sheared off his head.

It's a dangerous city. Kaliope finds herself being searched thoroughly, large white men tracing the curves of her body with metal detectors as she attempts to board streetcars, enter the library or go to the washroom. Even as she guides her bicycle west onto Oxford, she manages to attract appreciative attention. She swoops south, travelling against the traffic on Augusta Avenue, through the congestion of Kensington Market, past young homeless and young entrepreneurs.

Kaliope's used to being approached by men attracted to her darkness, men radiating a sense of complicity, an assumption that any contact between them is going to do both parties a world of good.

Sixteen-Year-Old Ruth

Racco, on the other hand, the all-white kid, radiating her pale beauty, often endures a defiant rage, as if she has always already made clear some fact of superiority and must be knocked back into place.

Ruth is treated as if she owns too much of her beauty, necessitating theft.

Kaliope's abundance of beauty is, instead, regarded with a socialist eye and considered, by some, a public asset for all to share.

Ruth Racco is looking to live a life that connects her with the happening streets of that pubescent city. She feels she should fit right in, charming the populace on the wheels of steel.

'Music is my lover,' she is fond of saying.

She's looking for a universal groove, something that everyone can, somehow, in whatever small way, relate to. A feeling that would be satisfying to all. She has been trying a variety of neighbourhoods all afternoon, looking for a place to spin, her records itching to jump their crate. She stands on street corner after street corner, sweeping her chest like a radar dish: Bloor and Spadina, always teetering on the edge of tawdry; Queen and Spadina, everybody and their shopping bags; Dundas and Ossington, just on the cusp of something but not quite yet.

A universal groove is something she feels she should be able to identify; it must be somewhere. Or more or less of it, anyway.

A universal groove, she reasons, would make you fall into it, so you just have to look for the feeling of falling.

She stands on Nassau, one of the side streets in Kensington Market, in front of the Happy Bean, a small café, and looks for a fullness that could make her round like a ball, a fullness so full she would simply tip over and roll, like an egg, falling through everyday life and everybody in it.

It's summer. It's beautiful. Life can, for the moment, be enjoyed.

The sound of a helicopter thunders in, disparate sirens converge and a black man, ripped with exhaustion and covered in sweat, stumbles past Ruth, trips and falls into the window of the Happy Bean, his shoulder shattering the glass. Police cars appear, spewing cops who pull the fugitive out of the jagged frame, blood from his forehead streaming into his eyes. He's cuffed, punched, then shoved into the back of a cruiser which peels off, its sirens screaming. The chopping of the helicopter fades into the distance.

There are fugitives, in one sense or another, everywhere; fleeing has become a global hobby, a typical way of passing an entire lifetime.

If you place your attention in the centre of your chest, you can probably feel yourself fleeing from something.

Some say there's a generalized flight from inadequacy, but that, in itself, seems an inadequate rationale, and not too many people want to get too close to it. Flight, in whatever direction, inspired by whatever privations, is, some say, the thing that fuels the thing maintaining the conditions that necessitate flight.

It's a tangle.

Ruth watches as the proprietor of the Happy Bean deals with the cops and begins to sweep up the glass.

'Hey,' says Kaliope, pulling up on her bike. 'What happened?'

'I'm not really sure,' says Ruth.

'Want to go for a swim?'

How Different Do

you think people can get? Is it too much to say some people, while fully in front of you and in the flesh, live in different dimensions?

No, of course it isn't. They do. People can operate in dimensions so different it's not much of an exaggeration to say they live on different planets.

If you like, it's possible to take a look at how your own world is divided into dimensions.

A dimension is most easily located in feeling. Look for the space between your different zones of feeling; they can be easy to spot – look for when a good day turns bad or vice versa. Moving from one dimension to another is similar to the operation water employs to turn to steam. In a particular dimension, things will flow in one way – your day will be easy, for example, or difficult. There will be a uniformity in attitude toward your life, and the world will take on particular attributes only apparent from that particular angle. It may feel simply like different feelings, but in reality they are different places. Once you find the dimensions, you can give them names. Watch how you cycle through them, or they through you. Try to use that cycle as a source of energy and predict the future. It's easy. And once you've mastered that, try to control the future.

We live on the period at the end of every sentence. We have whole cities – worlds – down here. But, on the other hand, we are also spread everywhere throughout infinity itself. Or so some say. Nobody's too sure what's going on – down here at the level of the period or out there at the level of infinity.

But, still, it's a beautiful day in that sad and sexy city, a bright day, a super day, yet, for some reason, the city continues to feel its loneliness. It wishes it were other cities: Chicago, New Delhi, Istanbul, Mexico City, Montreal, San Jose, Algiers, Moscow, London, Karachi, Caracas, Tokyo, Kathmandu, Barcelona, Bogota, Cairo, Perth, Berlin, Kinshasa, Manila, Singapore, Shanghai, San Francisco, Brussels, Paris, Seoul, São Paulo, Stockholm, Rome, Marrakech, Sarajevo, Cape Town, Lahore, Taipei, Athens, Prague, New York City, Casablanca, Kiev, Madrid, Nairobi, Dublin, Tijuana, Lisbon, Hanoi, Calcutta, Baghdad, Tel Aviv, Hong Kong, Santiago, Bombay, Copenhagen, Addis Ababa, Los Angeles, Helsinki, Kuala Lumpur, Las Vegas, Tel Aviv, Colombo, Havana, New Orleans, Mecca, Beijing, Managua, Jakarta, Oslo. It stares in wonderment at the fun those cities seem to be having. It wants to hang out late at night, too. It wants to drop out of school and have a coffee in the centre of all sorts of action; it, too, is itchy to fuck. It wonders if maybe it isn't wearing the right clothing.
It's not like that's never crossed your mind.

Ruth And Kaliope Float

in Alexandra Pool, snug at Bathurst and Dundas – Kensington Market with its confident anarchy to the north, Queen Street and all its slickness to the south, the Alexandra Housing Projects – a community under the cops' guns – to the east, and, to the west, a drive-thru McDonald's offering itself 24-7, if not more.

The pool is fifty yards long, outdoors – a simple affair presenting its surface to the wide-open skies of the metropolis, the water thick with bugs and band-aids. The sun casts a fruity meringue onto the underbelly of the clouds, smiling down to be reflected in the water.

Music dances across the pool's surface, a tinny sound emanating from tiny speakers meant more for announcements.

The influx of refugees from America is causing anxiety among certain members of the public concerned that services such as pools, parks and drinking fountains will be overrun by the newcomers. Proof of residency is now required in order to swim. Security is heightened and the lifeguards are issued pepper spray.

Kaliope feels the gaze of the lifeguard scanning her body, his pale eyes holding only enough green to not be grey. She looks up at him, high in his chair, overseeing the pool.

She looks away, then dives directly, headlong into the pool, the water thick and warm like saliva. She exhales, emptying her lungs, the weight of her body drifting downward, the blast of the lifeguard's whistle in the distance like a dream barely remembered. Little tornadoes of silt swirl on the floor, strands of hair hang suspended and leaves cartwheel along the bottom. She settles and sits quietly in the murk, her arms buoyed from her sides, the space between her cells expanding.

The underwater world offers an insulated version of life: all conflicts muted, gravity's power challenged. The bodies of others appear in the distance as mere blobs with almost no identifying traits, features fuzzy, the colour of the skin and a flash of a swimsuit the only things to offer themselves up to description.

A small sense of need circuits through Kaliope's body as she begins to crave air. She tries to distinguish the corporeal desire from her own, attempting to witness the concern in her veins, looking to draw a line between the needs of herself and those of her body. How can she ever be free if she is always finding herself bossed around by baser instincts like breath?

Transcendence may offer what might, at first, appear to be a solution, but it still depends for its very existence on something to transcend, leaving it, also, involved in a sad relation to superior powers.

Even the act of choosing, the very definition of freedom, leads to a reduction of options; finding a wall to pound your head against might just mean you won't be pounding your head against the floor. Maybe there's a winning lottery ticket lying on the floor. How would you know?

Air is necessary and will always insist on shoving its way into your body no matter how hard you resist. Is there any mileage at all in differentiating that which you call yourself from that which you call your body? It seems, Kaliope thinks, a question to be addressed only after death. But what exactly is death's target? Is the body the only thing standing in the way of freedom?

And, like death, can love, too, be interrogated for some answers?

Death in the end might just be easier; it will speak volumes eventually and inevitably. It's love that refuses to talk, or at least talk clearly.

Spasms pull insistently at Kaliope's diaphragm, her throat contracting. Fear grips her thirsty cells, but still she resists, her eyes shut against her body's nagging demands.

There are always big demands on a body trapped within a myriad of reflexes. No matter how much autonomy you might manage to carve out in a life caught in the crossfire of desire, your pupils will still defy any attempt at control and, if the light is bright, will contract no matter how you feel about the issue. Your heart will pump with or without your permission, your teeth will decay, wrinkles will etch their way into even the most advanced of your thinking, and a hand placed on a hot stove will demand removal with an urgency impossible to ignore.

The need for air makes one final tug at Kaliope's diaphragm before ceasing altogether, leaving behind, suddenly, no trace of any sort – no need for anything. Only waves of sensation – the water around her body, the bouncing of the dusk's light, the sound reverberating from other swim- mers – and the feeling that the top of her head has suddenly opened, like a camera's aperture, and Kaliope has become attached to something massive and decidedly feminine, the feeling startling her out of her reverie as she breaks through the water's surface, gasping for air.

The lifeguard blows his whistle and shouts a prohibition against diving.

Ruth swims to Kaliope.

'My head just opened – ' Kaliope's face is wet and very close to Ruth's, her breathing deep and laboured. Their noses almost touch, a drop of water on the tip of each fusing suddenly together, forming a tiny bridge.

'Really?'

' – and attached itself to something big and female. It was beautiful.'

Kaliope ducks under the waves.

Ruth pushes backward, floating, looking skyward and remembering that, being on a planet in the middle of space, she isn't looking upward but rather outward; there is no upward. The planet rotates on an axis, that much is true, but north could just as easily be south, as easily as you could be someone else given the right circumstances. You are only you because certain things have happened to you.

Maybe.

The warmth of the pool bleeds upward, the line distinguishing the water from the air blurring, creating the impression that flight is a matter merely of swimming uninterrupted from one medium to the other, up, out and over the city.

'Was I a part of this big female thing, too?'

'I don't know.'

And then they kiss. Lightly.

The pool keeps quiet, sloshing under the darkening sky. Or maybe it coughs into its hand with a burble. Not embarrassed, per se, but a little excited, the cough a release of a sudden bubble of interest.

But one thing is certain: something has happened and Kaliope's head did open.

'Whether Or Not

it has any meaning is not important,' Kaliope tells Ruth over a couple of lobsters at a downtown steakhouse located at the top of a fine hotel. 'What is important is that it happened at all.'

Ruth lifts a glass of white wine. 'To the feminine.'

'To the feminine.'

An hour later, the meal tucked into their stomachs, the two slip out of the restaurant and into the accumulating evening. The bill sits on the table unpaid. The other waiters organize a fund to cover the loss.

It's a simple reminder that the world is organized to rip off the people who, even for a moment, turn their backs on those they serve.

You've got to watch those you serve – they'll try to get you every time.

'That's the lesson,' says Ruth.

'That's the lesson,' agrees Kaliope.

'Explain It Again,'

says Ruth as she lies in the dark of Kaliope's bedroom.

'It was huge, actually – forever. But not forever in the sense of time,' Kaliope explains. 'Forever in the sense of distance. It went on forever. Not merely large, or vast, but complete. Everything. Eternal.'

Ruth's hand glides across Kaliope's stomach. 'I love touching you gently.'

'Did you know,' says Kaliope, 'that the origin of the word "gently" is the same as the origin of the word "gentrify"?'

'And "genetic"?'

'No, that's "genesis."'

'What about "genital"?'

'That would be "genesis," too.'

'And "genius"?'

'"Genius" traces to "genie," or attendant spirit.'

'Ghost?'

'Ghost.'

Shhhhhhhh.

The moisture that glistens on the bodies of the two girls is composed of the sweat of both as they lie skipping along the surface of sleep, buoyed by a crackling that still engulfs them. A lone bird begins to speak, its voice clear through the silent dawn.

The two girls try to outrun the morning, but the sky insists on brightening, knowing that while here it may be the night's turn to sleep, on the other side of the globe there are those just tucking in to their own sessions of lovemaking.

The bird continues to chirp.

A dustball curled in the corner shifts and, without so much as a breeze, makes its way to the centre of the room to get a better look at the two girls lying enraptured on the bed.

The bird's chirp stretches, bends and plucks itself like the strings on a violin. Both the girls see it.

It's blue.

Someone Has A

dream: two people walk toward a desert, bright with hot sand. One of the two people steps onto the shifting sands, which suddenly give way and swallow this person entirely. The second person moves to save the first, sinking fingers deep, like a pirate digging desperately for treasure. The head is discovered, the skull feeling raw as fingers are secured around the jaw and occiput. There is the fear, with the rest of the body sunk deep, that the head might just snap off or become dislocated, the soft cream of the vertebral discs popping apart – like a jelly doughnut, a little big bang. Universes begin; so must they end.

As the body is lifted from the earth, sand dribbling out of the head's holes, the ground gives way yet again and the second person is engulfed, each tiny grain on its own so smilingly insignificant but, inhaled as a mouthful, the majesty takes your breath away.

What can you swallow that will not, in turn, swallow you whole? The earth can slam its way into your body, as can the oceans, and, of course, fire finds you with no defence.

But remember *air*; air will always be the friend you forget you have. Nothing can go wrong there. Breathe it in and breathe it out. In air you trust.

But what can't swallow you may not be able, either, to hold you. Keeping yourself clear of the dangers of being consumed only leaves you vulnerable to the dangers of falling.

Hold tight or learn how to fly.

Kiss yourself.

Why not?

No one's looking.

Just put this book down for a moment and kiss your own
hand. Why not? What have you got to lose?

0

1

2

3

4

5

6

7

8

9

10

It's A Sunday

afternoon. Eleven-year-old Michael Racco and eight-year-old Rani Vishnu sit on the patio of the Happy Bean, a café in Kensington Market which offers a variety of coffees infused with essential oils, the caffeine shooting the herbs through the body.

Rani inhales a deep spray of the gingko biloba–infused brew across her tongue, evenly distributing the dark liquid across her taste buds. Michael does the same with a ginseng-bolstered number. Together, they talk about the phenomenon of pedophiles.

'I find they often look at me with appreciation and a desire to play,' says Rani. 'There may be some who want to hurt us, the same type who would be inclined toward rape, but then there are some who want merely to enjoy us.'

'The power differential is too extreme!' says Michael. 'To enjoy us is to hurt us. Anyway, this is about evil. I don't have the time to get bogged down by the particular versus the universal; I could blow at any moment.'

'You're just a little kid, who do you think you can achieve power over?'

The two stare at each other. The patio becomes inchoate, their eyes the only things in the vicinity. A dog barks in the distance. Rani smiles. 'Don't worry about me.'

Michael snorts, a look of fright passing over his face like a helicopter's shadow.

'You know,' says Rani, 'my uncle touched me.'

A moment slips by.

'How was that?'

'Confusing.'

Michael nods. 'My uncle told me that hot-dog wieners give him hard-ons.'

Another moment passes. Rani takes a sip of her coffee. 'They say coffee was first discovered by goats in Ethiopia.'

Michael takes a sip of his. 'In school we are urged to drink it. Our teacher was looking for improved classroom performance and had shares in some company in Brazil. What's that necklace?'

Rani touches a small cylinder on a leather string. 'It's from my dad. It's filled with a few espresso beans, for those times when I'm feeling unfocused.' She offers her cookie to Michael. 'You want a bite?'

'Is it peanut butter?'

Rani nods.

'It will kill me.'

Rani lowers her voice. 'Do you ever think it's romantic?'

'Romantic?'

'A desire to be intimate beneath a banner of mutual respect.'

'Uh – '

'Or do they just want to fuck little bodies?'

'Well – '

'Because sometimes I get the sense that it is romantic.'

'Michael, my good friend.' James Hardcastle appears, sipping his saw palmetto–infused latte. 'Here's the plan: it involves air. Any guesses? I'm sorry, have we met?'

'James, Rani. Rani, James.'

James extends his hand. 'Hardcastle. Pleased ta meetcha. Feel free to call me Jim, Jimmy or Jimbo. And you are Rani … who?

'Vishnu.'

'Ahhhh! Vishnu! The deity of destruction.'

'Love, actually.'

'Potato, potahto.'

'You're thinking of – '

'Of love, as usual. You watch out, Miss Vishnu, this kid is genetically predisposed toward acts of – well, let's just call his father flamboyant, shall we? Is that a chai latte?'

'It's an Americano,' says Rani.

James smiles. 'My favourite.'

'And the plan?' interrupts Michael.

James winks. 'It's easy, baby – I've got to get famous.'

'You are famous.'

James face grows taut. 'Fame is a boat with a very big leak. The bigger the fame, the bigger the boat; the bigger the boat, the bigger the leak; the bigger the leak, the more you have to work to stay afloat. Anyway, fuck water. The next mission: O_2.'

'Air?' asks Michael.

'I've walked on earth, fire and water, why not air?'

'I don't remember fire.'

'A hot stove as a toddler, no big deal – you've got CEO motherfuckers living on coals. But now let's talk about air.'

'You mean flight?' asks Rani.

James is stopped in his tracks. 'Well, I guess, yes, yes, it would be flight. Huh, how about that? I'm going to fly. Well, I'll be. I thought walking on air was gonna get me some press but flight – !'

Michael points at Rani's head. 'You have a grey hair.'

'I have five.'

'I need height,' says James, sitting down at the table. 'I need some serious height.'

'Height?'

'Height, like two-storey height.'

'You could jump off the roof of my building,' says Rani. 'It's nice, we've got a garden.'

'How high?'

'Well, like you said, two storeys.'

'Okay, okay, now we're talking. And I need a bedsheet.'

'For a cape?' asks Michael.

'A cape? Michael, this is serious business; you may very well have to catch me!'

James's Original Walk

over water had taken mere seconds and that's all he would need in the air, a few seconds – the few seconds it would take you to walk from where you're sitting to the closest person to whom you feel attracted. Look around you – people are beautiful.

A Big Dog

tied to the low fence that delineates the patio begins to bark, the animal's owners, a young couple with an infant, having just settled at the adjacent table.

'Sweetie!' the young husband calls to the dog. 'Quiet!'

'The miraculous,' says Michael. 'I don't know if you can plan for it.'

James looks at the Michael. 'Nobody's planning for it.'

'You can maybe make space for it, but what you're throwing down is a gauntlet,' continues Michael.

'Listen, space can be measured both by volume and by intensity. Intense moments simply occupy more of the landscape. Issue a new video game and you'll have the whole country talking, but blow up a building or two and you'll have the universe on the phone.'

'And jump off a building?'

'Well, I'm sorry – if the miraculous doesn't recognize a ripe opportunity, then there's nothing I can do to help it.'

'Because you don't know how or because you'll be in the hospital with a fractured skull?'

'Because I can't, Michael, because I can't. Look, I am trying my best here, people. If I can prove that gravity is not the be-all and end-all, I think we might see some very significant changes.'

The dog moves her head, the loose flesh of the leash letting go of the fence with a small sigh.

Now, Say You

are a dog just for a second. What might that be like? Say you are a dog, a dog owned by a young couple with an infant, a dog named Sweetie. What might you be thinking? You could be thinking this:

'These people with children, they seem to have some kind of access to a kingdom of shining bright. There's a feeling of holiness attached to this act of procreation. It's miraculous, there's no doubt about that, but it's as commonplace as the bees in the trees. Why does the blinding sheen of the sacrosanct seem to imbue all their gestures?'

Sniffing at an old, dried pizza rind lying on the road, you, the dog, Sweetie, might venture:

'Maybe because it's one of the only things that still connects these creatures to nature. It's an animal thing and they feel so pleased when they manage to nail it. It may not prove the existence of God, but it at least provides another person with whom to share in the suffering of that mystery.'

'Sweetie!'

There's a squawk of tires on pavement, the honking of a horn, the yelp of a dog and a car lurching to a stop.

'Sweetie!' The young father stands, while beside, in a stroller, the baby wails.

Out on the street the dog is quiet, its body having been bounced a few metres from the front of the vehicle. A fly buzzes the animal's ear.

The young father lifts his crying child while keeping his attention on the street. He calls again to his dog.

'Sweetie!'

Together with his wife, the man moves quickly from the confines of the patio, off the sidewalk and out into the street.

Rani, Michael and James watch, occasionally sipping their coffees.

The driver of the car steps out of his vehicle.

'The dog just walked in front of me.'

'Yes, of course.'

The young mother bends to touch the animal. A twitch ripples the fur.

From behind the car, a honk sounds.

The father steps toward the dog. 'Let's get her off to the side.'

'We should try not to shift her,' says the driver.

The woman moves toward the café. 'I'll get a piece of cardboard.'

From behind the car the honk resumes, holding longer. Then three short insistent blasts.

The driver glances back and gestures for patience.

There's another honk and then a piercing yell, causing James to choke on his latte, foam squirting out of his nose.

A very agitated man strides alongside the stalled vehicle.

'Move it!' the man shouts at the driver.

'I'm sorry, sir, but it's going to take us just a second.'

'Move it! Move it! Move it!'

'Please, sir, calm down, we just – '

The man throws a punch at the driver and the two begin to scuffle.

James turns to Michael. 'Was your father this apoplectic?'

'No, he was more focused.'

The man tosses wild punches at the driver, who slips on the dog's corpse, managing to avoid a knockout blow which accidentally lands on the head of the infant in the father's arms.

The young father calls out and frantically examines his silent child. Blood appears.

The young mother, holding an empty box, runs onto the street.

'Oh my god! Oh my god! Oh my god!'

The young father looks up, his eyes huge with terror.

'Call an ambulance! My god, call an ambulance!'

The woman fumbles for her cellphone, opens the device, lifts her finger to dial.

On the curb, the sunshine bright in his young face, steamed milk frosting his fuzzstache, stands young James Hardcastle, his arms raised high above his head, the tips of his fingers appearing to graze the clouds.

'Well, You Saved

a dog, that's something.'

Tears and snot drip from James's weeping face as the kids sit back and sip their cold coffees.

'I was showing off,' he sobs. His decision to build dramatic tension by first focusing a miracle on the dog is one he feels he will regret for the rest of his life. 'That little child will never know the joy of being alive.'

There's an awkward pause.

'Well, Jimbo, you know, life ... I mean, honestly, I never really notice the present unless I'm unhappy, so when I'm unhappy it's always the present, so I have the feeling that I'm always unhappy!'

James wipes his nose with the back of his hand. 'Is that supposed to make me feel better?' He shifts in his seat, reaches into his back pocket and withdraws a vibrating cellphone.

'So,' Rani says to Michael, 'you don't experience your happi-ness?'

'No, I only remember it.'

'But you feel it, don't you?'

Michael shrugs. 'I don't take note of it, which leaves me half as conscious as the unhappy times, thereby making those happy times half as real. Being unhappy is actually where it's at; you're less likely to make a stupid mistake because everything is noted and considered.'

'It's your sister.' James passes the phone to Michael, then grabs a napkin and blows his nose.

Rani touches James's arm. 'Life is a miracle, but is it really something to lament the loss of?'

'I've had some good times.'

'I've had times when I've kept the bad times at bay.'

Michael passes James the phone.

'What's up?' James asks.

Michael's forehead tightens. 'My mom tried to kill herself.'

'Is she okay?'

'I guess – she's at home sleeping.'

'We should go,' says James.

Michael shrugs. 'She's sleeping.'

'We should be there when she gets up.'

'Even when she's up, she's not really up.'

'Stop being so selfish and give me the keys to your house so I
don't disturb her with the doorbell.'

Michael stands and stares coldly at James. 'If you touch her – '

'If you don't have the compassion to – '

' – you'll fucking fly, all right.'

'Now, Michael.'

Michael sits. 'My sister is there.'

James stands. 'Oh, good, a threesome.' He winks at Rani.
'Ciao.'

'Romance ...' Rani resumes as she and Michael gaze off into the
Sunday afternoon café bustle. 'From all indications, it looks
to be a deadly affair. My first and only encounter with the
subject occurred in Grade Two. I fell in love with my teacher,
Miss Peach, and when she accused me of stealing one of her
pencils, an act committed out of love not malice, I fled the
school and spent the night hiding in the pet store at the mall.
I was arrested and charged with trespassing and theft.'

'For stealing the pencil?'

'No, I spent the night sleeping with a hamster, which I accidentally smothered. The store insisted on pressing
charges.'

'What happened?'

'Apologies all around and I was off the hook.'

'I was in love with my father.'

'Oh, yeah, I was in love with my father for a spell, too.'

Michael shakes his head. 'Irreconcilable.'

Rani nods hers. 'Completely.'

Jimbo Arrives At

the Racco home with a bottle of red wine. Ruth is sitting at the kitchen table.

'She's sleeping.'

'When a mother has given up on the world, her children experience a specific kind of dread.' James rummages through a drawer.

'Are you talking about yourself?'

James smiles and lifts a corkscrew. 'It's just something I've noticed.'

'What kind of dread?'

James purses his lips and impales the cork with a series of quick twists. 'Well ... it's silent and heavy; it doesn't suck like the deadly whirlpools of career and social anxiety.'

'No?'

'No. It lies on top of the child like a blanket soaked in blood.' James grips the bottle between his knees and slowly begins to ease out the cork. 'The imagined consequences are amorphous – they have no face – yet the whole thing feels terminal. It's like being abandoned to a sterile whiteness.'

Ruth traces her fingers along the skin of her arm.

The cork makes a quiet pop as it leaves the bottle.

'No offence.'

'None taken.'

James retrieves a couple of glasses from the cupboard.

'Was there a note?'

Ruth pushes a piece of paper across the table.

It says: 'Without family there is famine, and I would rather die suddenly than starve to death of isolation. I blame no one.'

James inhales the wine's bouquet. 'I've got this whole five-year plan.'

'Uh-huh.'

'It started with walking on water, then it moves to air – '

'Flight?'

'Sorry, flight.'

'Yeah?'

'And then once I've thoroughly proven that humans are not limited by the constraints of gravity, I intend to prove that racial identity is just as false.'

'Uh huh?'

'It's still on the back burner but – ' James leans in close to Ruth, ' – I'm calling it Project Chameleon.'

'I'm listening.'

James lies his left arm across the table, underside up. He touches the soft pale skin. 'I'm going to attempt to produce melanin at will.'

Ruth shrugs. 'That means nothing to me; I have no melanocytes.'

James winks. 'Mere detail.'

The Television's Flickering

light dances across the dark walls of the basement family room, playing on Ruth's face as she lies sleeping on the sofa: shots of the CN Tower as it rests in the lake and a party to celebrate the opening of the new restaurant that has been salvaged from the remains of the old. Very expensively dressed people lift snacks from trays carried through the crowd.

In Katherine's Bedroom,

James sits in a chair and stares at her as she sleeps. He stands and looks at her, his heart pounding and his breath short. He steps toward her and lifts a trembling hand. He touches her shoulder.

'Mrs. Racco?'

Katherine does not stir.

'Mrs. Racco, are you awake?'

Katherine remains inert as James reaches out and gently pulls off the comforter. Katherine lies naked, her pubic patch dark and full.

On The Television,

a representative of Citizens Against Road Rage (CARR) is extolling the virtues of Racco Radar, insisting it be installed at every intersection, in every mall, at every airport, in every high school, perhaps one day given to every employer, a home version developed so every parent can monitor every child, every spouse and every pet.

Little Eleven-Year-Old

Michael Racco and little eight-year-old Rani Vishnu sit down to a meal at a picnic table on the roof of Rani's warehouse as the sun agrees to set, leaving space behind for dusk and the occasional star with the strength to beat the city's bright lights.

Michael lifts the curried kingfish to his mouth, chews for a moment, then stops and speaks around the mouthful of food. 'Oh, shit.'

'What?'

'Are there any peanuts or peanut-related products in this food?'

'I don't think so.'

'Well, if I fall over, you might want to find some epinephrine. I'm always misplacing mine.'

After the meal, Rani gives Michael a tour of the dark roof.

'We're going to have tomatoes, carrots, basil, potatoes, pumpkins, cauliflower, broccoli, some sunflowers, cucumbers, green onions and eggplants.'

The two kids sit in the area of the garden designated as the pumpkin patch. The humidity holds them tight, their little lives bound by air and water, snuggled into the earth, waiting, maybe, to ignite.

The problem with fire is it devours that which provides it life. Fire, no matter how bright the burn, is never forever. In fact, the brighter, the briefer. Sound familiar?

'Is James really going to fly?'

'Who knows?'

Michael, unaccustomed to the particular spices of their meal, farts. 'Excuse me.'

'It's okay.'

The odour hovers in the air.

'I don't mind my own smell.'

'I know what you mean.'

'There's something reassuring about it, delicious even.'

'But the smell of others is disturbing.'

'I've sat for hours in public washrooms trying to determine if the smell is actually worse or if I'm revolted simply because it's not mine.'

'It could be a terror of the intimacy that the smelling of others engenders; the soft contents of their insides do, after all, have to brush up against an olfactory bulb as real as a tongue.'

'I wonder – if you were to inhale the odour of yourself while mistaking it for another's, would you experience a revulsion?'

'And, conversely, would another's foster the same ease and enjoyment if you thought it was your own?'

Some Say That,

so long ago, there were decisions made based on the composition of the king's stool.

That sounds about right.

That which is cast aside will always tell you more than that which is maintained. Who you're not is a more informative indicator of who you are than who you are has ever been.

So some say.

However, if constipation is your situation, it's probably a matter of working up the courage to take a long serious look. Then things will probably flow. You might be the type to read a book while on the toilet – well, that's fine, just don't be surprised to find the writing on your wall to be totally unrecognizable.

You must pay attention. You, humans, you.

Now, Back Again

with Rani and Michael. The two little kids, alone and on the roof in the garden, both squatting and grunting onto pieces of paper, their noses plugged so as not to skew the results of their research.

The experiment commences with Michael shutting his eyes and Rani sliding the two packages around like she's running a shell game. This is followed by Michael sliding and Rani smelling.

Do you want the details? Probably not. Are you feeling over-whelmed? Underwhelmed? Just nice and evenly whelmed? We can offer you little in the way of explanation. What's in a stink? How does a stink work? Who stinks? Do you stink? You often can't tell. It's not something you can even control. It's decided by other people.

James worries about foul breath. He worries about it often. It's what he considers a hobby.

'There's only one direction breath can go and that's bad,' he once observed. 'The receding of gums creates crevices into which food falls, is trapped and rots. There is no other way through it.'

But we're not talking about breath. And we're not talking about James.

On the roof of the warehouse, little eleven-year-old Michael Racco opens the first package and inhales. He nods and does the same with the second package, then slides them both to little eight-year-old Rani Vishnu. She repeats the small ritual, squinting her eyes as the odour singes her small nostrils.

'It's sweet. Sweeter than I expected. Sweeter than I

remember.'

'Yes, both do smell very sweet.'

There's a shudder of silence, a moment of dizziness. Michael closes one package, Rani the other.

'Which do you prefer?'

'Well, uh, you know, I've sort of lost my bearings.'

'Yes, I'm finding it hard to focus.'

'Would you like an espresso bean?'

'Please.'

Rani reaches to her throat, opens the small metal cylinder dangling around her neck and passes a few beans to Michael while crunching some herself.

'It did smell like shit.'

'I guess.'

'But the sweetness.'

'Yes, I'm still stunned by the sweetness.'

And, Later,

back at the group home, James's room is dark. The boy struggles in his sleep, attempting to drag himself awake. He dreams of a wall downtown in the back alley running parallel to Queen Street. It's illuminated by the light of the moon and James is just able to read the graffiti that covers it. It says: 'My name was Xiang Pao. I came here to find something better. I have been tricked. Life seems full of tricks. There are things that I was told when I was a kid and most of those things have proven to be false. As a teenager I was told a whole new set of things. A few of the past lies were cleared up but in the end they were simply exchanged for a new set. Now I'm lost, hungry and cold. Send help.'

And, Much Later,

someone has another dream. It's a simple dream, in which refrigerators are placed atop each other, rising high into the sky – a massive stack, reaching straight out into space, continuing forever, across light millennia. In addition, the refrigerators are empty and the stars are hungry. *Feed us*, the stars call, *feed us*.

There Have Been

times in the history of the world when it's been necessary for people to flee for their lives. Some say it's always that time somewhere or other.

Say it's that time right here right now.

Say you're a person who needs to flee.

No, don't say that, that's too easy. If you're a person who has to flee, either you have to flee or you don't have to flee – the question to flee or not to flee will always be answered for you by others. In most cases it's not a question. That's the problem with flight.

Say, instead, you're among the people who don't have to flee – the people in whose name whatever is being done to those who flee is done.

Do you remember the great underground resistances of the past, when people harboured others or shuttled them to safety across dangerous borders? Do you fancy yourself the kind of person who would rise to the occasion? Would you risk your life and liberty attempting to secure the same for somebody else? Do you think you would be able to recognize when the time is ripe to roll up your sleeves and get serious?

Maybe it's that time right now. Are people clamouring to get to where you are? Is it because the shopping's better?

In some circles, shopping has a bad reputation, but the energetics of the situation are magical: repetitive and mundane gestures performed over the course of the week are converted, in the off-hours, into objects that provide an outline for the trajectory of your life. It's a miraculous development.

Some are afraid of the marketplace. But there's nothing to fear. Not really. Not as such. Certainly some markets are dangerous – able to eat you like a cookie – but, really, that doesn't have to be the case.

Let's Say It's

July. The weather is hot and humid. Humidity is something you can call home, something that hangs around the street lights and gives a soft glow to the city; it airbrushes your life.

The city lies there, hot and wet and willing. It knows, more or less, that it has genitals, but it hasn't really figured out what to do with them. The place is so fresh it hasn't even stumbled on to masturbating. In its defence, in the lifespan of a city, these kinds of things take decades, centuries even. Still, like most teens, it's a horny city. A sticky city. It's a city on the prowl in the most innocent of ways. And, there's no doubt about it: Saturday night feels good.

It's a hot Saturday night. The humidity finds itself trapped between people and their underwear. Kensington Market makes the shift from day to evening to night. Fruit is pulled back inside stores, bins filled with a colourful myriad of dried goods are shut and locked, fish shops are swept out onto the street, lights are extinguished one by one and shoppers drift gently home, no one able to move too quickly through the thick air.

The dark rises, creeping out from the cracks in the sidewalks, seeping up from the earth to link with the sky. The street has been walled off from the sidewalk by stacks of boxes filled with rotting fruit. Cyclists roll their way slowly down the street, leaving a hazy wake, while music eddies on a sluggish breeze, floating around the corner from a café.

The owner of the Happy Bean, a young woman named Kate, got a loan to open the place and applied her education at a local design institute to create a warm living-room atmosphere. Relaxation, community and confidence-building form the core of the café's mandate.

Sixteen-year-old Ruth Racco stands behind two turntables, her headphones against her shoulder as, one night a month, a dance floor is cleared and people drift in after the internet café next door closes. Ruth lifts a mug and sips a cappuccino laced with camomile to ease anger, restlessness and impatience – the caffeine pushing the herb to do its job.

Sixteen-year-old Kaliope Vally sits at the bar sipping a frankincense espresso, advertised as being helpful for obsessive states linked to the past, while young eleven-year-old Michael, alone in the centre of the café, holds a cup spiked with cedarwood, a tonic for the kidney and indicated for states of unfounded fear. He stands there and searches for – but is having a hard time finding – a groove in which to lose himself. This makes him a little nervous.

In the washroom at the back of the café, little eight-year-old Rani Vishnu examines her head for grey hairs. She counts seven: two new ones since her arrival in the city.

Back at the turntables, Ruth watches her younger brother, Michael, and tries to forge some sequence in the music that will pull the little kid in, lift him up or just get him going, her vinyl spinning a web into the fragrant air of the café.

Kate, the Happy Bean's proprietor, believes that while you can't escape the company of yourself, you can make yourself so big as be unrecognizable. She believes that your sensation of your self is an actual landscape – a real geography, as real as the streets surrounding you. It is, she believes, like a maze.

Some say – she sometimes says – it *is* a maze.

It works like this: you are a maze. Throughout the course of the day you stumble upon particular aspects of yourself, tucked and hidden around various corners of you, and these aspects climb onto you and into you like a virus, infecting you with particular points of view, feelings, attitudes and biases. And you may recoil or relax. You can pull away and get away, pull away and stay stuck, or just let whatever happens happen.

Eventually, the phase passes and you stumble into another of the maze's zones to be consumed by yet another aspect of yourself. Often you'll stumble into the same aspect of yourself for days on end, struggling to get free, until, eventually, you do, that aspect disappearing and being replaced by others – the whole cycle repeating itself as, one day, you inevitably turn a corner to rediscover that aspect you had thought you had escaped all those years ago.

These phases occur in complicated elliptical cycles – mappable only by a science too sophisticated for symbols.

Think of yourself as a haunted house of mirrors littered with rotting bodies; you flip over a corpse to check its identity, and, time after time, it will be you – never quite fully dead.

It's just like that. Or it *is* that.

Kaliope Gets Up

and dances toward Michael. Michael dances a little toward Kaliope, then spins and faces the washroom door which opens to reveal Rani backlit by soft incandescence.

Rani dances toward Michael. Kaliope moves in and the three move together, Ruth matching beat after beat.

A few kids, attracted by the activity, wander into the café and order coffees, watch and wait to feel enough of the groove to fold themselves in.

Kaliope leans in close to Michael, her lips brushing his ear as she speaks above the music's friendly din.

'Have you seen your mom?'

'You mean, since – ?'

'Well, yeah, since ... '

Michael shrugs. 'She's mostly sleeping.'

A few of the new kids in the café step forward and begin to dance. The bell above the door tinkles as more enter, caught and teased by the groove Ruth is slicing.

The tincture-infused coffee provides all with a blast of harmony in one configuration of organs or another, knocking down walls in the maze of the self, the body's various parts functioning like a steam organ's pipes, the tincture managing to direct the force of the coffee toward particular combinations. If, say, the liver, lungs and lymph are amplified, one particular harmonic will be sounded, or if the kidney, intestines and blood, another; and the subjective experience is simply a shift in attitude – drastic or not so drastic.

James Hardcastle steps into the café. Michael raises his arm to wave hello. Accompanying James, stepping into the café herself, is Katherine Racco, Michael's mother. Ruth's mother, too.

There are dimensions in which everything is okay, in which things fit together nicely, make some sweet sense and look to be part of a thickening and strengthening process. These dimensions sit right on top of what is already happening, the dimension in which things are not okay, this dimension here. Or near here.

What *is* isn't the only thing there is. There is always plenty of room for what *isn't*.

What *isn't* sits on top of what *is* like an elephant sitting on an egg.

What *isn't* dictates what *is* much more than what *is*, itself, does. What *is*, is, in fact, simply an active reflection of what *isn't*. And not just any *isn't* but a certain *isn't* or, in reality, a whole massive group of *isn't*s.

*Isn't*s controlled by global interests.

'My feeling is that life possesses a massive potential which lies dormant.' Katherine sips on a juniperccino, feeling her kidneys strengthen in response to the tonifying berries.

'I thought you were depressed,' says Michael.

'Well, isn't that depressing?'

Little Thirteen-Year-Old

James Hardcastle stands in the café's washroom squeezing out a thin hot stream of urine. He groans.

'I've got a little inflammation in my prostate.'

Michael leans against the counter. 'How'd you get that?'

'How would I know?'

'How's my mom?'

James tries to manoeuvre past the little boy.

'Excuse me.'

Michael steps aside. 'I said, how's my mom?'

'Why are you asking me?'

'I thought you might know.'

'Michael.' James touches Michael's shoulder. 'My friendship with your mother should, by no means, come between you and me or, most importantly, between you and her. We're all adults here.'

'No, we're not.'

'Maybe not now, but think of the bigger picture.'

'I thought you were going to Nunavut to get Xiang out of the ice,' says Michael.

'You got a thousand bucks you can lend me?' James walks out of the washroom.

Michael stares at himself in the mirror.

He tries to see his eyes move as he looks away from himself.
Rani appears in the doorway.

'I'm trying to see my eyes move.'

'Can you?'

'No.'

Outside The Washroom,

in the café, things are heating up; a loose group of people dance in the centre, while Ruth leans over the turntables, her body a relaxed metronome. Kaliope sits behind her and flips through a small crate of records. She lifts one out and hands it to Ruth, who throws it down and sends it spinning. Music pumps out of the speakers, filling the room like smoke.

Katherine and James slip onto the dance floor, into a groove, joining the others in the centre of the café. Kaliope hands Ruth another record.

Back In The Bathroom,

Rani and Michael look at each other.

'I can see you – right? – see what you do,' says one.

'Right,' says the other.

'In many ways, I see you more than you see yourself.'

'Yes, I believe that's the case ... '

'I see your body betray you with glances or nervous gestures or whatever.'

'Right.'

'I can hear you.'

'Most definitely.'

'I can hear your voice change under the stress of the things you have a hard time saying.'

'Yes, absolutely.'

'Both to others and yourself.'

'Right.'

'I smell you, too, in a way that is beyond your own senses.'

'You will know when I have bad breath while I will likely remain completely in the dark.'

'I would say that's often, if not always, the case.'

'I can feel you with my hands, feel when you're tense, while you may not even have noticed your jaw is clenched and your shoulders are up around your head.'

'Yes, that can happen.'

'What about taste? Can I taste you more than you taste yourself?'
'I don't think I've ever tasted myself.'
'Me neither.'
Music floats down the hallway toward the bathroom. The tap drips.

Back In The Main Room,
Kaliope hands Ruth another disc. Ruth holds it aloft and gazes over the dancers toward what seems to be a soft red fog. Kaliope shifts and, too, notices the fog – the girls experiencing something between hearing, seeing and feeling.

By the way, it's almost impossible to distinguish your refuse from the refuse of another human being. That's just a fact of nature.

Kaliope hands a disc to Ruth.

James sits back, enjoying his coffee.

Kate, the proprietor, dims the lights.

Ruth turns up the tunes.

Personality Is Born
of the body. The interaction of the musculature, the organs, the fluids, the nerves; the whole apparatus humming at particular frequencies produces who you are. Who you are, in turn, determines how you radiate outward to others and how you feed back into yourself, this, in turn, shapes your body's structure.

Those of us without a rack of bones upon which to hang strings of flesh manage to manifest through a process of piggybacking. In order to experience what those with bodies call consciousness, we, without, tap into a multitude, working with one person's heart, another's bowels, another's brain, another's bones, constituting ourselves by way of specific configurations of individuals, this configuration always shifting, never the same from one moment to the next. Calling us an 'us' is both an oversimplification and an overdetermination, but it's probably the easiest way to describe the situation.

We can talk to you, as we are doing now, but only because you can listen: without you we're nothing. But we have no fears of abandonment. Abandonment is impossible. Just like we can't leave you, you can't leave us. Even if you put down this book and walk away, like the effect of a stone tossed into your being, we are ripples that, while we may disappear, live on in your forever-altered current.

And Then Let's

say it's much later. Let's say it's three in the morning. And let's say the water is cool – fresh, like lettuce.

And let's say Rani, Michael, Kaliope, Ruth, James and Katherine, covered with the sticky sweat of dancing, are scaling the fence at the Alexandra Pool to grab an illegal late-night swim.

The pool is smooth and deep blue, the orange sodium light scintillating on the surface.

Initially, the water grips and shivers them all – their bodies sensitive, nerve endings raw. After a few moments the cool blue is a balm.

James chases Katherine out of the pool and around the concrete deck, the two sprinting in circles, breaking the first rule of public swimming. Michael and Rani, both a little nervous, hover in the shallow end, sharing their nascent knowledge of swimming strokes.

Another boy and girl scale the fence, a couple of kids on the border between youth and adulthood. They say hello, strip down to their underwear and slip into the water.

Katherine grabs James and tosses him, laughing, into the pool.

'Your mother seems to be feeling better,' says Rani.
'Yes, she does,' says Michael.

In the deep end, Ruth and Kaliope float.
'Teach me how to open my head.'
Ruth stretches out, face down, and hangs there, her arms and legs limp. Kaliope follows, their heads bumping slightly as their bodies bob.
The water becomes almost all – the sound, sight and sensation against skin: everything.
Almost everything. There's also the air behind and above, cool on their backs but very far away. And there's the fact of the structure around them: the concrete, the grates, the tiny tornadoes of silt swirling on the bottom.
There's also each other as a bubble of awareness forms.
The feeling strengthens, until only one sensation remains and is shared, registering all the data processed by the combined efforts of both nervous systems.

And What About

these two other kids, the two new kids who just scaled the fence? Over there, attempting handstands in the water.

The girl's name is Grace Ng. She's seventeen. Her mother's parents are from South Africa and would have been considered 'coloured.' They immigrated as young newlyweds and fostered a strong and successful family. Grace's father's parents had come from China and were both successful within the health-care industry. Grace's father is athletic and has made a good living working in film, first as a stuntman then as a stunt director, and her mother owns a pharmacy. Grace is considered gifted; she has a huge brain and a voracious appetite for experience. She never really appears worried.

Gustavo Aguirre, the boy, also has a knack for maintaining his cool. He's seventeen, too.

His parents' parents came through Switzerland as refugees from Chile. He's a big guy and is thinking of becoming a lawyer. He doesn't view himself as white and is frustrated when anyone else does. He goes to great lengths in his speech, mannerisms, dress and hairstyle to prove he isn't.

He has a huge brain, too, but his appetite for experience, though just as strong, contrasts with Grace's.

Grace wants to experience a lot of different things while Gustavo is hoping to experience one thing fully.

Freedom, Gustavo says, and Grace agrees – freedom's what she's after, looking for it through unmitigated experience, while purity of communication is what he seeks, a telling of the truth, not as he sees it but as it is. Some things can be proven to be so: there's the hiding machine, the apparatus keeping everything hidden by a variety of operations.

And fame, too – fame, he feels, is real as rain and particularly irritating.

What's a revolutionary to do about fame?

Gustavo is a video artist and enjoys a certain amount of celebrity within certain circles. Grace is a filmmaker known to hold the fading art close to her heart.

Gustavo understands the confines of reality and knows that a good many of them are, for now, immutable. He doesn't want to change anything as much as to slip beneath everything.

'Disappear into the interstices and then, like water, freeze, cracking things apart,' he sometime says.

Or he wants to be the rot that attacks the root of the tooth. Why not? Only a few people are able to be a president of the United States and everybody knows that – just like there are only a few people who would be able to assassinate a president of the United States, no matter how badly the rest of us want to, need to, how hard we would work for it.

But everybody can rot the root. It's easy. And, surprisingly, it's fun. Most of the time. Or, it looks a lot like fun, and these days there is little difference.

Or so Grace would say. She wants to take pictures and tell stories about the human soul. She feels there is width and breadth to this thing, not to mention expansion and contraction, thin and thick, dense and diffuse and, of course, deep and shallow. It's like juggling hundreds of balls.

Gustavo, on the other hand, is interested in deception and power. One of his early video pieces, *Plain Clothing*, created a stir; he developed his own facial-recognition software, hid his camera outside police stations and throughout some of the city's more happening neighbourhoods and captured, collected and cross-referenced images of people who worked for the force but only appeared in the public in plain clothes. The cops shut it down, but not before the images had been disseminated all over the internet.

Rest assured, there is a file somewhere with Gustavo's name on it.

Maybe you've got your own file. You'd be surprised who does.

And Over Here,

in the deep end. Here are Kaliope and Ruth, still floating, trying to find the place where their heads leave off and everything else begins.

If we had to represent the interaction occurring between the two girls, it might look like this: '.......................................'

They communicate in what might be a series of ellipses. There is something about the whole thing that is finite, finished and certain but still maintains a great deal of ambiguity.

And what about you? Okay, look, it's easy. There you are. The book is in your hands. All the letters on this page are shining information into your face, to be scooped up by your eyes and fed into your body.

Your chemistry changes in response to what you read. Your very system is altered, the flowing of the fluids and the humming of the organs changes. You can feel it if you pay close enough attention. Check it out: place your attention on your body and notice the feeling in your stomach as we flash by a couple of words.

Cunt.

Cock.

Did you experience a physical change? It might be subtle. You have to be very attentive. Perhaps those particular words don't really resonate. What about:

Fame.

Fortune.

Anything? Maybe something a little more specific might work for you:

Mommy.

Daddy.

Well, either you've noticed it or you haven't.

If you are so inclined, you can wonder whether or not, as we enter you, you enter us.

That's a good question.

The answer is complex and it's mostly no – no, you cannot enter us. We can enter and follow you, with our presence not *entirely* affecting what you do, but *enough*. Though it can also be said that you, in some ways, bring *us* to life. It is through you that we find expression. Another way to think of it is that you collect us like a solar panel collects light, but our light, like so many of the stars in the universe, is something you capture long after our deaths. We're dead. Like, really dead. We're not here. You're all alone.

But in that aloneness there's lots to harness, lots to do, lots of potential to realize, with or without us.

Maybe we're trying to reconstitute as something else. That would be our best guess. Isn't that what everyone's doing?
There are some zones where you can just *be*, but they're rare and appear to be strictly off limits.
Rumours abound as to why, but no one has been able to come up with a satisfactory story.

Here, try this experiment. Look around for the nearest person; when you've found them, watch them very carefully and we'll jump from you to them.
Go ahead. Put the book down and look carefully for the nearest person. Walk around a bit, if you have to. And when you've found them, just look at them. Discreetly. We'll make the jump. Once we get there, we'll signal you somehow.
Try to look for us in how they move, what they do with their hands, head, feet. We'll find a way to be a part of that movement as a signal to you we've made the transition.

Check it out. We'll meet you back here.

Well, either you did or didn't. What matters is we're still all here together. Swimming in the pool. That's the important part.

0

1

2

3

4

5

6

7

8

9

10

The Demonstration Began

at the university in front of the doors of the research centre
that houses the team responsible for Racco Rage Radar and
is snaking its way down Spadina Avenue.

The cops are, as usual, everywhere.

There's a common notion that holds that the police have a
difficult job, but it has been well documented that
elementary-school teachers get injured more often than
cops do. The populace is quite adept at policing
themselves.

Kaliope and her aunt, Amina, hang near the back of the
crowd, eschewing chanting, preferring chatting, instead.

'I don't know – ' Amina says, pulling a mango out of her bag,
'I don't think you should waste your time with poetry.'

'Your life is not so bad.'

'Believe me, it's a carefully crafted illusion.'

'You're going to be famous.'

Amina begins gently kneading the mango. 'The only way for
brown people to get any press is to blow up something.'

Amina continues pressing the skin of the mango with her
thumbs, breaking the flesh until the fruit gradually resem-
bles a small water-filled balloon. She bites the nub at the
top, creating a small hole through which she sucks out
some of the liquefied fruit. She passes it to Kaliope.

'There are simple and efficient ways of doing things,' Amina
says, 'secret ways. Ways you wouldn't want to share with
just anybody.'

The demonstration winds its way around the eyeball bank
and turns left, continuing east along College Street.

Race And Racism

are the threads from which is woven the very fabric upon
which the world treads. There is often, if not always, the
question of how to move without walking on this ground.

There are strange clickings on telephones, snippets of
random conversations, echoes, feedback and laughter.
There is the sense that nothing can be said that isn't being
overheard. While this may not be true, it certainly could be
true. There are listening devices everywhere. Communication is always being intercepted, sorted, filed and shared.
Everybody knows this.

Some say that the only thing race is good for is to divide the
population into work categories. Those who wash the
dishes will be Sri Lankan, those who drive the cabs will be
African, those who run the banks will be European, those
who watch the kids will be Filipino, those who mind the
store will be Korean and those upon whose bodies the good
life is modelled will be, more and more, a hybridization of
all of the above – on TV, on billboards, in magazines.

But it would be a mistake to believe that these beautifully
mixed people represent a race-free future – that people will
stop their fixation on difference and settle down to enjoying similarities. It's just a smokescreen. Part of a dazzling
performance. And there's no way to fight it. Or maybe
there is – it's a matter of expanding the powers of the
imagination.

You can imagine that a chirping bird in a nearby tree reads
your mind; it does, after all, seem to be chatting with you,
so why can't it be so? You can forget everything they told you

as long as you've got someone willing to feed you soft food.
Why chew at all?

Kaliope Imagines

there is a large hole growing in the centre of her face. She
imagines the hole widening so all that remains is a narrow
band of skull creating a circle through which, as she walks,
the breeze will pass. She imagines dipping this circle into
soapy water and, as she marches down the street, leaving a
trail of lazy bubbles wobbling in the air, bubbles filled with
all the terrible thoughts she can't stop thinking, floating up
over the city to burst high overhead, sprinkling the populace, evenly distributing her anxiety: a socialism of angst.

Kaliope has a flash of eye contact with a couple of people who
look familiar to her and who may look familiar to you: the
two doing handstands at the pool the other night, Grace and
Gustavo, each carrying a camera – Gustavo with video,
Grace with film.
Kaliope glances their way and they glance at her, then they all
three look away without acknowledging the recognition, as
if the small contact at the pool has never happened.
As we've mentioned, that's just how things work in that
shy city.

The demonstration crosses Bay Street and stops in front of
police headquarters, some people gathering in the courtyard and some on the street. Amina and Kaliope hang in
the middle. Cops on horses hang at the back.
Amina points up toward the building's main doors, located
at the apex of a triangle formed on one side by a sheer wall

of glass that cuts in on an angle from the street and on the other by the adjacent building. 'You'll notice that to get to the doors you have to climb these steps,' she points to a complicated zig-zag, through which cuts a flowing fountain, 'and cross that bridge, the water acting like a moat.

'And over there,' Amina points toward the east side of the courtyard, 'there's the wheelchair ramp, protected by two railings. The steps, moat and bridge make it impossible for a mass of people to get to the door, and the wheelchair ramp functions as what's known in chess as an "open file," designed to allow cops to move quickly down out of the building to position themselves behind anyone who might have gathered.'

'How do you know this?' asks Kaliope.

'Well, look at it, it's obvious. And that sculpture,' Amina points to a bronze image of a female cop, holding a trowel and leaning over a pile of stone bricks, which dominates the middle of the courtyard, 'is placed to stop a crowd from forming a nucleus.'

A woman at the top of the steps near the bridge is speaking into a megaphone. 'Racco Rage Radar is a violation of privacy and is being used by this racist police force specifically to target our communities – communities that have every right to be angry.'

A commotion erupts on the periphery of the crowd.

A female cop confronts one of the protesters. 'What kind of mother are you?'

'I'm sorry?'

'Bringing your child here.'

'Fuck you.'

The female cop pounces on the woman, grabs the child and calls for reinforcement. Cops shove their way into the demonstration.

'Give me back my baby!'

'She spat at me,' says the female cop.

'My baby!'

The crowd starts to shout and shove the cops, chanting 'Shame, shame, shame,' over and over.

On the other side of the crowd, a number of cops move in and snatch another kid out of a mother's arms.

There's a couple of popping sounds and canisters of tear gas twist furiously in the crowd. Equestrian cops swing their riding crops down onto the heads of the demonstrators. People are pinned in the courtyard.

A panicked man, trying to avoid a horse, scrambles up onto the pile of stone bricks. He approaches the summit and slips, rolling backward and falling beneath the horse, which rears in panic, dumping its rider onto the bronze sculpture of the female cop, the trowel catching the rider's neck. Blood sprays across the crowd. There are terrified screams. Riot cops savage the crowd, encircle the injured officer and pull him in. Another canister of tear gas twists between Kaliope's feet, spinning and billowing its poisonous fumes. Cops randomly chase down panicked people, slamming knees into backs, pinning people to the ground. Other cops descend, securing their arms with restraints and punching heads.

Blinded and gagging, Kaliope stumbles onto the street, trying to pull away from the chaos, searching for Amina.

The City Holds

the sense that everybody could be doing significantly better. There is talent, determination, lots of good ideas, but, for some reason, something is interfering with the city's ability to make a leap forward. Some say it's simply a lack of cold hard cash.

However, while there may not be the monetary resources to move the thing forward, there is enough dough to keep the population intertwined with circuits of energy that have been there for years and years.

The city is like a teenager who can't have access to the car until it does its chores. And there is always another chore.

Is the future as much of what *is* as the past?

It is. That's the remarkable thing. Just like the past, the future can be a partner, a friend. It can also be a weapon.

But if you don't have the strength to wield the future, you should find something else to do: take out the garbage, wash a dish once in a while, filter some water for the rest of us to drink – make yourself useful. Or if you're really feeling crippled by the current state of affairs, then, by all means, miraculate yourself. There are miracles occurring all the time, small ones and big ones – miracles are a dime a dozen. Take the afternoon off and become one. What's stopping you?

João Da Silva Had

arrived in the city in 1973, his family fleeing the unrest in Angola. He had wanted to open his own grocery store along Dundas Street but couldn't secure the financing, and, instead, his father's brother's wife's brother had set him up with a construction job. On April 26, 1973, his first day of work, João slipped and fell into the still-wet foundation of the CN Tower. His body was never recovered.

The CN Tower, formerly the world's tallest freestanding structure, was finished in 1976. Some say ghosts haunt the place and it was they, not some crazy tornado, that lifted the thing up and dropped it into the water. But that's ridiculous. Maybe there was some help from the ghosts, but a bunch of wisps couldn't pick an apple off a tree, let alone topple a building.

It's just not how things work.

Do you have trouble focusing? We do. Is it a sign of the times, do you think, or simply our nature? In any case, there certainly seem to be a lot of possibilities wrapped up in what might be described as our heart. Or at the heart of the matter. How is focus supposed to be attained? It's a tricky question. Is there really no system of orientation left? That's preposterous. There are some serious things that we can really know, important things, things upon which to base our focus. For example: up, down; more, less; over there, over here; breathing, not breathing.

Think about it this way: try not to think about it at all.

Up, down. You can definitely distinguish between up and down. And what more do you need?

The CN Tower, the tower formerly known as the world's tallest freestanding, is definitely down. Down for the count. Debate rages as to what exactly to do. There are two factions: those who want to raise the thing and those who want to see it used as the first leg in a walkway connecting to America: an outdoor friendship mall.

And, indeed, the structure is doing better business than ever, with people flocking to the city to visit the thing more than they ever had while it was standing. And the elevators continue to operate, bringing people horizontally to what used to be the observation pod, which, since the catastrophe, has been converted into a café and swimming pool, the lake water that flooded the building now filtered and chlorinated.

Those who want the thing resurrected talk often of national identity and invoke civic pride. Those who prefer to let the thing lie in the lake talk simply of fun. It's fun. It's fun to walk on, it's fun to sunbathe on, and it's fun to swim in. Some of the world's largest retailers are thoroughly keen to get aboard, their representatives openly lobbying for public support, appearing on talk shows, on public radio and at community forums, claiming that a percentage of the profits will go to programs to assist urban youth: it will be fun for everyone.

The Union of Elevator Workers, a bunch of guys who ride elevators all day long, can hardly be accused of not appreciating fun. But in moderation. Fun is fun, you can't argue against that, but to stabilize the future, sometimes immediate fun has to be forsaken for future fun. The union is prudent but can party. And they want the thing returned to its standing position. It means a lot to them. Many have been up and down that thing thousands of times. It's nice satisfying work, with a bracing element of risk, fresh air and an unparalleled view of the neighbourhood.

And it has become a symbol of what's possible for that

teenaged city, for that youthful country. It's a gracefully designed monstrosity, conceived at a time when to be a citizen of that sprawling nation was to be just on the verge of happening.

Height is very important. If you've got a little height, you'll find that, as people tip their heads back to look up to you, the blood supply is slightly pinched off at the back of the neck, resulting in sluggish thinking, delayed responses and a convenient docility. Try it: lift your gaze to the heavens and walk quickly around the city. No can do – you'll bump into things.

So the structure had been tall. Big deal. But a big deal it is. And leaving it in the lake is a betrayal not only of the city but of the entire country, so some say.

Others say the notion of nations is looking pretty ridiculous. New political configurations rule the day. In partnership, some say. But partnerships – the very idea, some are saying, has reached the end of the line. There must be a better way of thinking about these sorts of things.

Katherine And James Sit

at the café that has been constructed from the broken remnants of the revolving restaurant; with the tower tipped on its side, everything is available for new configurations, the walls functioning as floors, and bathers on either side, slipping into the water.

They sip cappuccinos.

'James, that's insane.'

'It only sounds insane.'

'You're thirteen years old.'

'I'll be fine. I'll dress warm, I'll stay in a nice hotel – '

'How are you going to afford it?'

'Well, that's exactly what I'm talking about.'

'And are you going to just walk everywhere?'

'Look, Katherine, just, like, five hundred bucks.'

'You should be in school.'

James stands up. 'Xiang's soul is at stake!'

'The boy's soul is not your responsibility.'

James slumps back into his seat and folds his arms. 'Five hundred dollars is nothing to you.'

'It's not about the money.'

'You know, I have half a mind to get a goddamn job and fucking make that money.'

'Someone your age can't just lounge around a Nunavut hotel.'

'I'm going there to do some serious work.'

'You'll have to deal with Children's Aid – just like here.'

'Fuck those pigs.'

'When you're sixteen, you can do whatever you want.'

'That's a laugh.' James drains the dregs of his cappuccino.

Katherine lights a cigarette. 'You're too clever.'

'Can you please order a glass of red wine?'

'James – '

'It's my birthday.'

'No, it's not.'

'It is.'

'Today?'

'Yeah, today.'

'Really?'

'Yeah, really.'

'Well then, happy birthday. Do you want some cake?'

'No, I want a glass of red wine, but because I live in a totalitarian state, I can't order it myself.'

Katherine looks at the boy, sighs and signals the waiter. 'You'd
     better not be lying.'
'Or what?'

You'll Never Know

it all. Most people die knowing about .0005% of everything
     there is for them to know. Most plants will die knowing in
     the neighbourhood of 5%, insects 2% and most other
     mammals 1%. This takes into account not only what you
     know but how you know it. Most people are like magazines:
     they know a little about a lot of things.

Intelligence is calculated according to a formula that evalu-
     ates that which you know, grading it according to its ability
     to – and this is the key – *drive toward fun*. Everybody likes
     fun, even if you're the type of person to find unhappiness
     fun, and intelligence is always trying to get you what you
     like.

The knowledge of things that are not fun only bolsters intel-
     ligence by virtue of providing an understanding of what to
     avoid in order to keep fun running. Plants are able to access
     more fun than humans because they are more intelligent –
     intelligence defined, again, as the interface between a
     thing and everything that's not the thing that manages to
     ensure fun.

When sitting in the sun is all you need to know to have a good
     time, then you're what we call smart.

The Police Helicopter

chops the sky into shards. The world curls around itself like a
     drunk teenager around the base of a toilet. Or maybe it's
     just the city curled around the lake, a smear of vomit across

its handsome chin. In any case, there is sickness every-where. The righteous have no problem seeing this. Unless you call madness a problem.

Are you righteous? A little?

It's true: these days, too much truth can cause you problems.

Kaliope Is In

the bathroom, vomiting. Ruth is in the hall, knocking.

'Are you okay? Kali?'

Kaliope's stomach strains to push its way out of her body, hoping it can escape and flop into the cool waters of the toilet, then further down the pipe, into the soothing lake, while Ruth's hand, yearning to heal, presses against the warm wood of the door.

'Kali?'

Kaliope vomits again.

'Unlock the door.'

The house is silent, holding itself pregnant, wondering if its water will burst soon.

'What's wrong?' Ruth presses her cheek against the door while the hard plastic of the toilet seat digs a groove into Kaliope's forehead. 'Kali?'

Exhausted strings of yellow bile stretch from Kaliope's mouth to the quiet water in the porcelain bowl. She reaches for toilet paper, wipes her chin, flushes and then lies on the floor.

Ruth abandons the door and retreats to her room, lies on her bed and stares at the ceiling.

Kaliope creaks slowly down the dark hallway toward her bedroom. Ruth's door opens. The two girls look at each other.

'Are you okay?'

'No.'

Kaliope goes into her room and shuts the door.

What about this: all those days ago in Kaliope's room when a chocolate bar came slicing across the floor.

Ruth opens the door and slides herself into the room.

'Is it okay if I come in?'

Kaliope remains silent, a tight knot lying on a tired futon. Ruth sits beside her on the bed, reaches out and touches Kaliope's back.

'What's wrong?'

There's sickness in the air, that much is certain, but there is also an anxiety. Everybody is always wondering where the fun has gone.

Ruth slides into the bed beside Kaliope, spooning her and stroking her hair.

'Don't.'

Ruth sits up on the edge of the bed. She jiggles her knee.

'What's wrong?'

'My aunt was arrested today,' Kaliope whispers.

'Your aunt?'

Kaliope is silent.

'In Detroit?'

'No, here.'

'You have family here?'

The sound of a distant helicopter bounces around the room, slicing the silence into small pieces. Kaliope stares at the dark wall illuminated only by the light trickling in from the street.

Ruth stands, moves to the window and stares out. The sound of the helicopter grows louder. Ruth looks back at Kaliope. Kaliope continues staring at the wall. Ruth searches the room for something to say.

'I was just reading this interesting article.'

Kaliope doesn't respond. Ruth continues.

'There's a guy who has spent thirty years searching for a universal groove – a groove that infects equally all who encounter it. He's searched all over the globe, he's amassed tens of thousands.'

Kaliope remains silent.

Ruth reaches down to the ground and picks up a page of the business section that lies on the floor. 'Why have you underlined this article? Why is this interesting to you?'

Kaliope speaks quietly. 'It just is.'

'How? How could this be interesting?'

'It just is.'

'What do you care about minerals in cellphones?'

'That mineral exists only in one place.'

'So?'

'That company,' Kaliope gingerly props herself up, 'hires mercenaries to terrorize the population.'

'What does that have to do with you?'

'Maybe I want to live there in the sun with people who look like me.'

The sound of the helicopter draws closer.

'We both have curly hair,' says Ruth.

'Yes,' says Kaliope.

'We're both beautiful,' says Ruth.

'Did you know?' Kaliope stands and moves toward Ruth. 'If you don't underline articles like that, the sentences in the newspaper detach, drift up and form creatures: the living embodiment of all the intentions of those who write the articles. And if you're not looking, they can strangle you. Did you know that?'

The sound of the helicopter grows thunderous, shaking the windows, gusts of air whipping in as light bounces around the bedroom. Kaliope moves cautiously to the window and looks down to the street.

A searchlight sweeps porches, and the movement of a man leaping over a fence catches the attention of the two girls. The helicopter thunders, the blaze of its searchlight smashing into the bedroom. The man ducks down an alley. Headlights slash the darkness as a van obstructs his path. Five cops jump out, grab the fugitive and drag him toward the vehicle. The man randomly glances up at the house, noticing Ruth and Kaliope, his face illuminated by the white light gushing from the sky: late twenties, dark skin, dark hair and wire glasses. He could be a computer programmer. He is cuffed, punched, then shoved into the van; the doors are closed and the vehicle speeds away.

The sound of the helicopter fades.

After a short silence, Kaliope turns to Ruth. 'What makes you think everybody is going to want to dance to a universal groove?'

'What?'

'Would you want to attend a party attended by the whole world? Doesn't a successful party require some people to not be invited? Isn't that half the fun?'

'You didn't tell me you had family here.'

'So?'

'What did this aunt of yours do that was so worthy of arrest?'

'You know, you've got to know who you're *not* to understand who you are,' says Kaliope, backing Ruth up toward the futon.

Ruth sits on the futon. 'But you know who you're not only by virtue of who you want to be.'

Kaliope moves in. 'Which is just another aspect of who you're not.'

Ruth stands. 'It's who you're going to be!'

'You wish.'

There's a pause, then Ruth slaps Kaliope hard. They are both surprised.

'I can be anything I want to be,' Ruth offers as an excuse.

Kaliope backs out of the room.

Ruth comes after her. 'I can.'

Kaliope moves down the stairs, gaining momentum.

Ruth follows. 'I can.'

Kaliope flies through the front door, down the steps to the sidewalk and up Euclid Avenue.

'You can, too!'

Is that true? Do you believe that's true? To a certain extent, maybe. But you can't be a turnip, after all. Or a victim of torture, just because you want to be. That's impossible.

The past is a hospice for dying regrets. They're fed through tubes. Let them die, some say; everything else has to, why shouldn't they. Forget about your regrets; unplug the machine, send for the undertaker or whoever needs to be called in an event like this. There was an article in the papers about a kid who drank an entire bottle of drain cleaner and ended up developing an exoskeleton. It apparently came in very handy. The little kid could roll down the stairs, flight after flight, without sustaining so much as a scratch. No regrets there.

Think of everything as a parachute over your head. You can reach up, grab it and pull it down. If you've got enough strength. Not strength in your muscles, although that helps, but other places.

The place you get your inner strength, though current conditions would have you believe otherwise, is through other people. That's the sad and confusing paradox of inner strength. It's not yours. It never was.

Kaliope Sits On

a bench beside the concrete wading pool in Bellevue Square, a dry twig of a park in the heart of Kensington Market. She stares at graffiti sprayed on the ground: 'Dem ah sistahs! Dem ah undastand.'

Ruth Lies Curled

in her bed on Euclid Avenue, a pillow on either side of her head. She empties her mind of all content. Trying to breathe it slowly out.

The sound of the police helicopter, now an almost permanent fixture, can still be heard in the distance, cold white shards scattering through the night, illuminating the world with a sick glow.

Someone Has A

dream: the city thunderstruck and ablaze 24/7/365. In basement apartments, carbon-monoxide detectors beep in distress and children collect the pictures of cancerous mouths that appear on cigarette packages.

Houses shudder violently in winds that lift newspaper boxes and send them, chains shattered, smashing onto the streets, liberated newspapers scattering in the wind, whipping high, low, skimming along the ground. People try to read their horoscopes on the fly, chasing their destiny as it zips along in the storm, some actually catching a glimpse as the newspaper twists in the wind, deking in and out of traffic, only managing to read a single sentence of the day's prediction – 'Love can destroy you' – before being run over by a streetcar.

But a working definition is in order, don't you think? You can't just toss around a word like that, during days like these, in a place like this, without generating a little something or other – confusion, or unnecessary debate. So let's work on a definition. Rani?

'Love?'

Yeah, kid, love; what's love?

'You can't say what it is but only describe the conditions under which it will flourish.'

Good answer. Rani awakens suddenly, her chest tight with some kind of agony, sad roots entwining her ribs and constricting her ability to breathe. The little girl gasps for air.

It's morning. A new day.

Congratulations.

0

1

2

3

4

5

6

7

8

9

10

It Is A

new day, a fantastic morning, a morning that holds the promise of luxurious heat.

Little eleven-year-old Michael Racco walks along the railway lines, down from the suburbs and into the city, his little sneakers clicking in the gravel.

Sixteen-Year-Old

Kaliope Vally sits with a cappuccino on the patio of the Happy Bean, her eyes still a little puffy from sleeping and weeping.

She doesn't necessarily believe in Allah as a sentient force who makes sure you remember to press the button before you cross the street but rather as a vague pattern, a stream, perhaps, or a current that can capture even the most banal occurrence and turn it into coincidence, like milk into foam.

In milk you simply sink, but foam's got some substance. Not enough to stake a life on, of course, but sometimes enough to calculate, say, how many times a rock might skip or a phone might ring or a dog might bark.

In a word, utterly useless. But maybe the Almighty is just having a bad day. In any case, that's just the way things are at this moment, on this day, in this beautiful morning sunshine.

Kaliope spent the night in her aunt's empty apartment, sleeping alone, curled up in a big wicker bowl in the shadow of a massive bookcase. Now, sitting on the patio, she gazes out, the memory of Ruth's slap, if not the slap itself, still tingling on her face.

Sixteen-Year-Old

Ruth Racco, on the other hand, lies in bed, her pieces drifting
together as she stares at the grey screen that occupies the
space between dreams. She is trapped in a maze, passing
corners and patterns of twists and turns; it all looks too
familiar, she's always taking the same route, pleading for it
to be different. Ruth touches the wall of the corridor and
feels the familiarity double back on itself and startle her
awake with the realization that not only will she never
escape the maze but she herself *is* the maze. It is the horror
of being pinned to the body of a dead person.

She moans as she shifts and slips back into the depths of
sleep.

Then There's Little

eight-year-old Rani Vishnu. She walks down the road, the sun
illuminating yet another grey strand on her head, the early
morning light bouncing off the hair and smiling to the world.

'Hey,' calls a voice from the patio of the Happy Bean.

Rani looks over to Kaliope.

And Where Is

thirteen-year-old James Hardcastle? Is he curled up in a ball
waiting for a bounce? No – no, suddenly there he is.

'Hi,' he says to himself. 'I know what I want and I know how
to get it. Even if it is just from myself.' The little kid smiles
at his reflection in the window of a passing store and winks.

Little Eleven-Year-Old

Michael Racco leaves the train tracks near the chocolate factory
where Dundas and College fuse and jumps onto a streetcar.

'What were you doing down on those tracks?' demands the driver.

'What?'

'Were you doing graffiti?' The driver lifts his phone. 'If I call transit security, you'll be in big trouble.'

'I'm more of a thinker than a doer. Look at my hands: they're clean.'

'Well, that's private property, you stay off it. You could get yourself pulverized.'

Michael pretends to deposit a token. 'I once saw a fox on those tracks,' he says.

'Really?' says the driver.

'It chased me for miles.'

All the streams of the past converge on the present. Everything that's ever happened to you, all the things you've learned, all the things you've thought, are squeezed together, tied up in the tightest of bundles, allowing you to pass through this tiniest of windows: this moment here.

Here.

If you listen carefully, you can hear the past pushing through the present like toothpaste through a tube.

And there are sparks – of course there are sparks. You can see the sparks of your past illuminate your present at almost every moment. Sometimes it's enough to ignite the hay you keep hidden in your skull. Luckily there's a lake nearby. It may not be clean but it's wet, and when your head's on fire that's all that counts.

Kaliope And Young Rani

sit together on the patio under the ascending sun. The coffee melts away the day's rougher edges.

'Difference is a shifty ground,' says Kali.

'It's a dangerous place.'

'It can be.'

'There's the difference born of an imbalance.'

'I've been told imbalance is the only way to achieve motion; walking, so they say, is just a matter of stopping yourself from falling again, again and again.'

'Can imbalance exist without gravity?' wonders Kaliope.

'Can balance exist without gravity?'

'And what about flight?'

'What about flight?' James sits down at the table with an Americano.

'Is falling a necessary component?'

'Well,' the boy laughs nervously, 'though it may not have to be, it has to be an option – otherwise it's just floating.'

'Hey.' Michael arrives and sets a latte on the table. 'Is it just me or does civil unrest in South America translate into bad coffee for everyone?'

'It's weak,' Rani agrees.

'Yes,' says Kaliope, pushing her cup away. 'It is weak.'

Imagine if a piece of fruit could be genetically altered to slice itself.

One day, don't you worry.

And your own genetic code manipulated to create a self-picking nose.

Anything is possible.

Back In Her Bedroom,

Ruth stares at the ceiling and imagines drinking a large amount of alcohol until she is so drunk she can't see straight. She imagines then swimming feverishly into the lake, continuing until she's exhausted, far from the shore, too loaded to notice as the water punches its way into her lungs – her pale skin, in death, finally making sense.

The phone rings.

When is the last time fame gave you a call? Even in the smallest of senses. Have you achieved any notoriety through your deeds? Do people you don't know talk about you? Are you often referred to by both your first and your last name?

The Stairway To

Amina's apartment is narrow and steep, reaching up to the third floor of a building on Spadina Avenue just on the edge of campus. Higher learning reverberates around that part of town, paradigms are knocked around, sometimes down. The bookstores nearby offer knowledge: a lot of old and a bit of new. Maybe, one day, long in the past, there was the feeling revolution might be possible. Who knows. The present wears the past like eyeliner wears tears.

'Right now,' says James, taking two steps at a time two steps behind Kaliope, 'we live in a psychic police state.'

'Uh-huh,' says Kaliope, taking out a key and opening the door.

'There's something always watching.'

'It's the desires of a few large white men,' says Kaliope. 'It's everywhere and you're just so surprised to see it because you happen to be a very large white boy.'

'Are you calling me fat?' asks James.

'I just think it's paranoia,' says Michael.

'But that's okay,' offers Rani. 'The most paranoid assumptions can still provide you with the basis for action. Most inaccurate information – even from the most deranged mind – usually misses the mark only along quantitative lines. The insane speak in metaphors and, like the rest of us, in stereo, so no matter how nuts you are you can usually figure out where you're at by simply triangulating between the worst and best things you can imagine.'

'And if you get lost?' asks Michael.

'You're never too far from boredom, so just wait until the next cycle.' Rani looks around the small kitchen.

James's cellphone buzzes his pocket.

'So where's this coffee?' asks Rani.

Kaliope opens the freezer and removes a few containers.

James hands the phone to Kaliope. 'It's Ruth.'

Rani, James and Michael explore the apartment, moving down the hall to a living room dominated by a massive bookshelf composed of boards and bricks, snug from floor to ceiling, completely occupying one of the apartment's walls. There are hundreds of titles, thousands perhaps, volumes that try to account for how things have gotten the way they have – books written with the blood of the people, the hidden history of the world, some would say, telling you the many things those who hold the key to the kingdom don't want you to know. The three kids stand in awe before this sheer cliff of knowledge.

Kaliope steps into the room with four steaming cups of espresso.

'Where's this aunt of yours?' James asks.

'She's not here.'

He pulls out a copy of John Porter's *Vertical Mosaic*. 'She's got a lot of books.'

'Put it back.'

'Yo, my hands are clean.'

'As an individual, maybe.' Kaliope moves to the stereo, lifts a record, slides the vinyl out of its sleeve and lays it on the turntable. The soulful butter of the Stylistics comes flowing from the speakers.

James sits down, lifts a cup to his nose and inhales deeply.

'Where does your aunt get this?'

'She's been all over the place.'

'I've heard about a coffee,' says Rani, sitting engulfed in the big wicker bowl. 'It's made from the very best beans, one in a thousand. The workers steal them a bean at a time and spirit them away under constant threat of punishment. They make a coffee that only they and their loved ones drink. And it's never sold.'

'It's never sold?' laughs James. 'Likely story.'

'Did you know,' says Kaliope, 'that coffee is the most-traded commodity after oil?'

Remember: there is someone being tortured right now. Odds are, anyway.

There are flying monsters circling, or so some say. Some say the wires that power the streetcars transmit a song from the future. Some say there's a shut door talking to you like you were its parent.

'Open me!' it whines. 'Open me!'

The doorbell rings and Kaliope quickly leaves the room.

'Balzac used to drink sixty-seven cups a day,' says Michael.

'The most-traded commodity after oil?' says James.

Kaliope steps back into the room, accompanied by Ruth. The two girls are tense.

'Hey,' says Michael.

'Hey,' says Ruth.

'You want some coffee?' says Rani.

'Sure.'

James addresses Ruth. 'Kali was just telling us coffee is the most-traded commodity after oil. Did you know that?'

Ruth shrugs and shakes her head.

James turns to Rani. 'You?'

'It makes sense.'

Then to Michael. 'You?'

'No,' says Michael.

'Neither did I,' says James. 'Why didn't I know that? Why is that not common knowledge? I mean, oil is obvious, right?'

'Absolutely,' says Rani. 'The world is scarred by that fact.'

'But coffee? Coffee?' says James. 'Who's involved in coffee?'

'The same people involved with everything else,' says Kaliope.

'I drink this every day!' exclaims James. 'My life must be structured by coffee at both its most cellular and geopolitical levels!'

'Calm down,' says Ruth.

'I didn't know that! What else don't I know?' the boy demands.

'Did you know the earth revolves around the sun?' asks Kaliope.

'Of course,' says James, sitting on the futon. 'Everybody knows that.'

'Did you know I'm going to be famous?' asks Ruth.

'What are you talking about?'

'I've got a sidebar in *NOW* magazine next week.'

'What?'

'A little article about me. And a list of my favourite public pools.'

'What's so interesting about you?'

'Well, my night at the Bean.'

James rises from the futon.

'For playing records?'

'Yeah, guy.'

'For playing records?'

'So?' says Ruth.

'All you do is play records!'

'Whatever – there's skill, people like what I do, it's important.'

'Important?' James screeches.

'It means a lot to them.'

'Important?'

'Yeah, guy, important.'

'I'll show you important!'

The boy rolls up his sleeves and storms out of the room, through the kitchen, out the back door and on to the porch.

'James!' Michael calls.

James steps on the Refugee Backlog, leaps onto the railing and hoists himself up and over on to the roof. Michael and Rani scramble after him.

Kaliope And Ruth,

left alone, stare at each other, the silence broken only by the sound of James's heavy footfalls on the roof and the Stylistics singing:

> *If I were a business man I'd sit behind a desk*

I'd be so successful I would scare Wall Street to death
I would hold a meeting of the press to let them know
I did it all 'cause I'm stone in love with you.

James Stands On

the low wall that edges the perimeter of the roof and looks
  down three storeys to Spadina Avenue. The bell of a streetcar roundly sounds its cheerful ding.

'Don't,' says Michael.

'You don't have faith in my abilities?'

'I don't really have faith in anything,' says Michael.

'What about you?' James asks Rani.

'I don't really know you.'

'You don't think I can fly?'

'I don't know what to think.'

'You think I'll just drop to the ground?'

'That would be my guess,' says Michael.

'I'm not doing this for me, I'm doing this for Xiang. It's a
  selfless act.'

'If you say so.'

'I walked on water.'

'You did.'

'I resurrected a dead dog.'

'You did.'

'If I pull this off, it's going to be Easy Street for me.'

'That's true,' says Michael.

'Yes, my friend, it's very true. The cake will cut itself if I can fly!'

James turns toward the street below, while, below him,
  through the roof, down in the living room, Ruth and
  Kaliope suck hard on each other's tongues, slamming
  across the floor like electrified lobsters, while directly

above, on the roof, James turns toward the street. He looks up into the sky and lifts his arms.

Down Below,

the two girls consume one another's mouths, their teeth clacking together like dice. What feels like a laser-thin wire composed of pure silver, blinding in intensity, seems to breach their clothing and attach their vaginas.

It feels great.

Opening their eyes simultaneously, they each catch a glimpse of their own reflection in the other's eyes. And reflected in the reflection of their own eyes is the other's face. And in the tiny eye of the other's face is a vision of the world.

Kaliope looks deep into the reflected reflection of Ruth to see something horrible. Terrible. Something like dead, bloated bodies: victims of rape, or poison, or bombs, or yet more torture. Perhaps chunks of flesh, or bleeding bullet wounds. All forms of betrayal imaginable, blinding sharp shards slicing into the optic nerve. Ruth, on the other hand, looks deep into the reflected reflection of Kaliope to see a beautiful world. Spectacular. Something like a world of comfort and caring, perhaps a world of dancing, laughing and swimming. A revolutionary world where tedium, fear and oblivion aren't the only options – a warm blanket of a world held confident in the arms, as easy as 1-2-3, as straightforward as A-B-C, as fundamental as 'you' and 'me.'

What's the most beautiful thing you can think of? Is world peace more beautiful than inner peace? Is inner peace more beautiful than a couple of weeks on a beach in a tropical paradise? What's the most horrible thing you can think of? Are severed genitals more horrifying than years of solitary confinement? Is solitary confinement more horrifying than being surrounded by people who laugh too loudly at their own jokes?

For the sake of our purposes here, let's just say it's that the girls see hiding deep within the reflected reflection in the eye of the other. Ruth sees your most beautiful thing while Kaliope sees your most terrifying thing. Or things like those things. And they immediately pull away from each other, the intensity of the vision shocking them apart, Ruth slamming into the wall, Kaliope into the bookshelf.

Back On The Roof,

James inhales and bends his knees, but is interrupted by the chirping of his cellphone.

'Excuse me.' He pulls the phone out of his pocket.

A massive crash shakes the building's very foundations. Rani and Michael look at each other and scramble down off the roof, leaving James alone with his phone.

'Can I call you back, Mrs. Racco? I think I'm in the middle of an earthquake.' The boy pauses. 'Sure, like in, say, half an hour? Cool. Ciao.'

He hangs up the phone and starts to move away from the building's edge. He stops, turns back to the street, looks down, collects a mouthful of saliva and spits. A sudden gust of wind pulls the gob down hard, fast, and then, just before it hits the pavement, the wind circles the saliva, rocketing it back up toward James. The boy instinctively opens his mouth and the spit jumps back in. James closes his mouth and swallows.

'Well, all right.'

Rani And Michael Enter

the living room to find Kaliope and Ruth trapped beneath the
rubble of what was once the bookshelf, the sound of the
shelf's collapse still reverberating around the room.

Kaliope moans. Ruth shifts.

Rani and Michael wade into the books and begin to dig the
girls out.

Ruth, in a daze, reaches out to Kaliope. 'I love you,' she slurs.

Kaliope recoils. 'No, you don't.'

Ruth crawls through the carnage toward Kaliope. 'I love you.'

Kaliope backs away, her eyes wide. 'No, you don't.'

'I do, I do, I love you.'

'No, no, you don't.'

Michael steps toward his sister. 'Ruth, maybe you should – '

'I love you, I love you so much!'

Kaliope presses her forehead against her knees. 'No, no, no,
no, you don't!'

Ruth tries to stand but slips on a copy of James Baldwin's *The
Fire Next Time* and crashes to the floor.

'Ruth.'

'I love you so much!'

'No, you don't!'

'Yes, I do!'

'No, no, you don't!'

'Yes, yes, I do, I do, I do!'

'You don't, you don't!'

'No one will love you like I love you!'

'No!'

'I will love you forever and ever and ever and ever and – !'

'Excuse me,' interrupts little eight-year-old Rani Vishnu. 'Love is not necessarily a good thing.'

Ruth tries to focus her eyes on the little kid.

'It's just a force. A force that simply accelerates the human mechanism. Two people who fall in love suddenly have access to twice the amount of thinking power, twice the ability to move through space, twice the sense of humour – twice as much of everything, but, keep in mind, they still have to choose which things they will think, which direction they will travel and which jokes they will find funny.'

'Is that coffee still hot?' James walks into the living room. 'What the – ?'

Ruth pulls herself to her feet and makes her unsteady way through the books. She pauses and turns back to Kaliope.

'My love for you will never die. It will be here long after I'm gone.'

Then the kid makes her unsteady way to the door and down the long flight of stairs, her footfalls reverberating through the building.

'There's nothing wrong with love,' says James, tossing back the remainder of his coffee. 'Well, sorry to drink and dash but I've got to go. I've got a date. Oh yeah, Michael, your mom says hi.'

James heads out of the apartment, leaving Rani, Michael, Kaliope and the pile of books.

'Are you all right?' asks Michael.

Kaliope nods.

'Here.'

The two little kids help Kaliope stand and together they push through the books and begin to reassemble the shelf: three stacks of three bricks – two in the corners of the room and one in the middle – across which they lay a piece of plywood, then continue alternating bricks and plywood until the structure reaches the ceiling.

As they begin to fill the shelf, warmth radiates from the books into their hands. The heat spreads, inching into their wrists, up their arms, to their elbows, up through their armpits into their shoulders, pouring down into their torsos, filling feet, thighs, groin, back, front, face, head, teeth and finally searing their eyes, which the three kids close while steadying themselves against the shelf.

And when they open their eyes they can see through walls.

Not really. They can't see through walls.

Or maybe they could, but just for a fraction of a fraction of a second and then the ability is no more.

They sit together on the futon, exhausted, satisfaction rising off their bodies like steam.

What constitutes your satisfaction? What could satisfy you here and now? Obviously there are different strokes for different folks.

Of course, you are satisfied with what you choose to talk about with your friends, otherwise you would just change the topic. Is there anything you don't know you're not talking about?

If you're asleep at the wheel, does the wheel care? Should it?

James Catches Up
with Ruth on the street.

'What's the rush, sister?'

'I'm not your sister.'

'Your mom and I are hooking up for some bean-water, care to join?'

Ruth grabs James by the shirt and slams him against a building. 'You owe me melanin!'

'Whatever, nigger, that's a future project.'

'You promised.'

'I said I'd do my best.'

'Well, get on it.'

'I got a few loose ends to tie up. Speaking of which, now that you're famous, can you lend me a thousand bucks?'

'Get out of here.' Ruth shoves James down the street.

'Whatever, dude, it's a free country. I go where I want, I do what I want, I am who I – '

A rush of rage consumes Ruth as she grabs James and hisses, her white face, filled with blood, turning a fluorescent pink.

'Is it?'

Confusion grips James's face. 'What?'

'A free country? Is it?'

'Listen, Ruth – '

'Do you feel free?'

'Ruth, I just bought this shirt!'

'Do you?'

'Free? No, I don't feel free. But only a thousand bucks stands between me and that sensation. So, either cough up or fuck off.'

Ruth stares at the kid for a moment, her breath condensing on his upper lip. She releases her grip. James straightens his shirt and rubs his throat.

'You've really got to do something about your temper.'

There's A Skull Staring

at all your plans.

It doesn't have to be a creepy thing.

Say there's a skull sitting beside you right now. At your elbow, on the armrest, or if you're reading this on an airplane, peeking out from the crack of the overhead bin. If you happen to be in your bed, look quickly, maybe there's a smiling skull staring out from the closet. Let's say it can talk.

'Hi,' it might say. 'Don't think you're going to live forever.'

Live forever, you might think, live forever? Who would want to live forever?

'So What's

up?' James sits with Katherine on the patio of the Happy Bean.

'I'm pregnant.'

A seagull wheeling overhead screeches.

'Oh.'

'Isn't that nice?'

'What does Mr. Racco say?'

'He doesn't know.'

'Does Michael know?'

'Your mom, Joan, is the only person who knows. She thinks I should keep it.'

'Of course,' says James. 'She did me a similar disservice.'

'Your life is not so terrible.'

'Ha! Look at this putrid world. Look at what passes for imagination! Do you think I like living in a shit factory?'

Katherine lights a cigarette and looks up at the seagull.

'Can I have a drag?'

'I should quit.' Katherine passes the cigarette.

'So, you're going to keep it?'

'Raising children can be a revolutionary act.'

'Since when are you interested in revolutions?'

'I've always taught the kids to share.'

'Some preparation for a world guided by greed.'

Katherine takes the cigarette from the James. 'My kids are fine.' She takes a drag and flicks it onto the street where it catches the slipstream of a passing car and is sent spinning in a shower of sparks.

Later That Afternoon,

Michael and Rani sit in the wicker bowl, held like pearls, while Kaliope sleeps fitfully, a knot on the futon. The sun is at the top of its arc in the sky and the air is dead with heat. On the floor are two small pairs of pants and two tiny pairs of underwear.

'How does it work?' asks Michael.

'The same as yours,' says Rani.

'I mean, where's the hole?'

'Somewhere here.'

Kaliope's snores are like velvet cream in the heat.

'Why is it so hard?' asks Rani.

'It's not always like this.'

'It's ticking.'

'I believe that's my pulse.'

Let's talk about the clouds that hang tired in the stifling sky, always so sad. There's a child on the radio singing over and over: 'Get yourself together. Get yourself together. Get yourself together ... '

'What the people don't know can't hurt them' is a maxim that lingers in the air around these parts, thick and oppressive like the humidity of a late July afternoon, strangling and smothering anyone who just wants to act like themselves once in a while.

And, some say, it doesn't get any better. It only gets worse, fascism and other stupid behaviour springing from the body's inability to freely feel itself. That's the theory, anyway.

Ruth, On The Other

hand, lies sobbing in Kaliope's empty bedroom, feeling fully, her face pressing into a warm pillow.

She has spent the day hallucinating Kaliope again and again in the bodies of other girls – girls walking down the streets or girls sitting at cafés. Sudden inhalations mark these mistaken sightings and leave in their wake a racing heart; the city is scarred by the mist of Kaliope's presence. In fact, if the truth be know, the city shimmers with the ghosts of both girls.

No big deal. The city is shimmering with you. With everyone. Always.

What Ruth and Kaliope have is true love. A new love. A new way of loving. Something that's supposed to change the world.

An important love. If it were a song it might sound like this: 'Zing zang, superduper, skies are blue for me and you.'

It has the world written all over it. It has tendrils that attach themselves to all the stuff there ever was, is and will be.

Some say the world is weeping, choking on sobs, unable to breathe, suffocating on its own snot. And while that may or may not be true, what is true is that Ruth is weeping, her tears soaking into Kaliope's pillow. Against her chest she clenches a newspaper she found while searching Kaliope's room for clues about what went wrong. On the front page of the newspaper is an article about the spread of one new virus or another.

Ruth considers that perhaps this virus was concocted to decimate certain populations. It could be true. Tweaking of genetics here and there could easily target particular people. The idea it could be true makes her weep harder. Rolling over, she allows the sound of her sobbing to fill the room; fragmented through the prism of her tears, she sees the dusty track lighting, focused upward, bouncing a soft ambience on the ceiling. In the glow of the light shimmers the shadow of a caught insect, struggling.

Ruth stands on her bed and reaches up her arm, tipping the lamp downward. The bulb flashes in her eyes, a small moth managing to escape as a collection of dry dead wasps cascades into her face.

And Even Later

in the afternoon, back at Amina's, the air in the apartment dead and still, dust motes hanging in the hazy late afternoon light, the two little kids have melted almost into nothing, their bodies now asleep while other parts of them – shards of their electrical underpinnings – squirt like fountains or jump and arc like lightning, until the phone breaks apart all the fun.

'Hello?' Kaliope rises groggily from the futon.

Nobody Is Really

surprised when the prosecutors, in the empty silence of a secret trial, produce transcripts of Amina's radio shows which, in the ugly light of the secure room, leave only the impression of a danger to the state.

Amina points out to the court that, considering the current situation, most of the world's population is opposed to the way things are. How can you fault her for interviewing the world's majority? She's just telling it like it is. The judge agrees: Amina and the state are indeed enemies.

0

1

2

3

4

5

6

7

8

9

10

A Little Kid

vanishes while walking home from her friend's place and the next morning pieces of her body are found wrapped in plastic and bobbing against the smooth concrete of the CN Tower. Her murder dominates the front pages of the newspapers as all the parties play their various roles: cops shoot off their mouths about being hot on the trail, the mother prays on her knees in front of the shrine that accumulates, the gathered photographers lift tumescent lenses, while concerned citizens from the neighbourhood stand in front of microphones and access the multitudes for the first and last time.

The location of the grisly discovery provides a smart segue for the newscasters as they move on to the conflict between the Union of Elevator Workers and the management of the CN Tower, a company whose PR flack points out that while the mechanism continues to operate, shuttling tourists out into the harbour, it, as such, can't be considered a device of elevation.

The general public is conflicted, the split somewhere around the nation's consistent fifty-fifty, half demanding, for the sake of the perpetually embryonic state of the national identity, that the thing should be immediately resurrected. Those who are content to leave it lying in the lake take to op-ed pages with the suggestion that since the United States is more than just a friend, the tower should be renamed the Family Bridge and extended to officially link the two sister nations.

There are some who view the Family Bridge as a step on the already crowded slippery slope to a loss of sovereignty. Others say sovereignty is long gone anyway. Why pretend?

There are more differences between individuals from different regions and cultures than there are differences between the two countries. Open the borders, some say. Mix it up. Get dirty. The national pretension, after all, is simply a way of focusing and controlling the minds of the masses. It's time – or so some say – to blow the lid off.

But nobody wants to go anywhere where there isn't a map.

To argue war is everywhere is easy. The military processes that are always conquering faraway lands and that, not so long ago, atomized the battlefield and, in turn, everyday life, into a series of gestures made by people unaware of the whole of their actions – this process is so deeply entrenched that most of the populace takes it as normal. In the militarization of everyday consciousness, truth lies bobbing in the water like a dismembered child, the lies everyone is always telling strung like used dental floss from light pole to light pole, from every awning of every house to the gutter of every life, making a thick web on which people slip, bits of one person's lies getting stuck on the bottom of another person's shoes.

Ruth Racco Rides

her bike up and down the streets of the city, through residential neighbourhoods and back and forth across commercial zones. She listens to the sounds of the city: the honks of car horns, the laughter of children, the happy dings of the streetcars, cement trucks shifting gears, sirens and the ubiquitous chopping of the police helicopter, a fixture as permanent as the sky itself.

One day both may fall, it's true, but there's very little point in
structuring your life around the possibility of such events.
You can hope, certainly, but don't let that hope distract you
from dragging your ass through the tedium of every day. If
the sky falls, it falls. If a new plague tears at immune systems
all across the globe, knocking this whole place off its rocker,
or a bomb or two renders a nice cozy apocalypse, then, all
right, all this will have finally made sense. But in the mean-
time, you're just going to have to keep on trucking.

Ruth doesn't view sound as something that travels then
enters her ears but, instead, as something that is always
there to be scooped. It hangs in the air like a shifting mist
and she moves through it, catching and collecting it. And
the colours, too, generated by the sound, hover like a mist
to be inhaled by the black pools of her pupils.
And if the sight of sound can be captured by her vision, the
sound of sight must be available, too.
Ruth moves like an albino bat through the world, searching
for Kaliope, looking to hear the sound the girl's skin would
make, entering environments with her body ablaze in
search of Kaliope.
Or anything resembling Kaliope.
Or, at least, not resembling herself.

Kaliope Has Been

vomiting all day. Her body aches. She wanders through her
aunt's apartment, looking at all the belongings left behind.
She rereads the letter Amina has sent through a lawyer:
*'When you see the flash of a fish glint in that dirty lake, a
bat at dusk in the sky; when, at the height of summer's heat,*

you hear the cicada singing its electric song or smell the first drops of a fresh rainfall on hot August asphalt, you will find me – I will be there. Always.'

Kaliope touches stacks of paper and art on the walls. She opens the refrigerator and stares at its contents; she curls herself into a sphere and rolls herself down the hallway like a bowling ball, careening into the bathroom. She flops open her arms and legs and lies on her back. She makes bubbles with her spit and blows them into the air. She commands the sink to turn on.

It doesn't.

Or does.

She stands in the centre of the living room and pretends to pull an arrow from a quiver, insert it into an imaginary bow and shoot it out the window, down and into the street.

Then she follows the arrow out, down the stairs.

Kaliope is certain that police cruisers follow her.

She believes she has an ability to think herself invisible. It doesn't always work, but sometimes is better than never. It does take its toll, of course.

Being invisible is, on the one hand, easy. It's as easy as holding your breath.

Try it. Hold your breath. It's easy.

Anyone can hold their breath. But try to keep holding it – that's where things get tricky. You stay invisible for too long, you'll die. Just like holding your breath.

Kaliope sometimes believes she is already dead. Why not? She might be. So might you. Everybody knows that.

There's the worst-case scenario you keep thinking about. And
then there's everything else.

No offence, but you have structured your life around
anticipating the worst thing imaginable. Which makes our
existence hell. And we mean hell.

Kaliope sits on the patio of the Happy Bean and stares at a
photo of the cop who was killed at the demo.

'They're going to come and get us,' Gustavo says to her.

The boy sits down in a chair.

'They already got my aunt.'

'Yeah, well, they're coming to get you. And me.' The boy
extends his hand. 'Gustavo.'

'My name is Kali.'

'Yes, indeed, we're going to jail.'

'Can I shoot you guys as you talk?' Seventeen-year-old Grace
Ng points her Super 8 camera at Gustavo and Kaliope.

'This is Grace.'

'Hi. I'm Kali.'

'Do you mind this?'

'Sure, whatever.'

'If you're uncomfortable – '

'No, no, it's fine.'

Grace begins to expose short bursts of frames.

'This is something you quickly get used to,' says Gustavo.

'What will you do with the footage?' asks Kaliope.

'I don't know,' says Grace.

'Win awards,' says Gustavo.

'Yeah, right,' says Grace.

'Grace has no faith.'

'They're just little experiments.'

'Did you see this article?' says Gustavo. 'This crazy elephant is getting tons of coverage.'

'It's a miracle,' says Grace.

'I drink milk every day. Nobody's coming round to take my picture.'

'I'm taking your picture right now, you idiot.'

'Oh, yeah. Cheese.'

'What elephant?'

'This fucking crazy elephant. Ganesh. It started in India a couple of days ago. One of his devotees had a dream where Ganesh was drinking some milk. So he fed some milk to one the statues and it drank it!'

'Really?'

'That's what they say. And now it's happening everywhere. All over the globe. Even here in Toronto.'

'In Toronto?'

'Yeah, right up the road. People are lining up. There are traffic jams. It's the real deal.'

Gustavo continues to scan the newspaper, reading an article about a group of scientists who claim that individuality is shared; the person you are depends significantly on the people you're with. Individuality, their evidence strongly suggests, is mutable, as permeable as water. People leak in and out of each other, swapping constituents and passing them into the ocean of humanity; this ocean, they suggest, could be conceived of as one thing, a distinct and discrete entity, knowable, quantifiable. Much of the scientific community is up in arms over these findings, the church, too, dismissing it as nonsense. The Pope claims that just because he understands someone else's joke doesn't mean he is that person. Lines, he insists, have to be drawn.

Is there anything you know you wished you didn't know? Would you want to know everything? If you knew everything, what would stop you from making an informed decision? Nothing. Wouldn't that be nice?

What if you already know everything but don't know you do? Wouldn't that be funny?

Are you laughing yet?

Grace continues to shoot Gustavo and Kaliope as they sit in the late-morning sunshine. Grace believes that the trick to accurately portraying the day is to see how close she can come to selecting edits in which nothing seems to be happening.

Life, she believes, is mostly a series of non-events possessing insignificant effect, but, when enough have accumulated, a shift occurs. Like an earthquake. It's the smaller things she wants to capture in order to string out a story that speaks of life as possessing the inevitability of a train wreck.

It isn't destiny she's interested in, but the tracks on which life travels. And these tracks, she believes, are simply the blinding everydayness of other people. She believes it is only between oneself and other people that the propelling energy gradually accumulates.

Have you ever owned a coffee mug that said, 'Today is the first day of the rest of your life'?

Out loud?

'Today is the first day of the rest of your life,' says Kaliope's coffee mug, but the girl isn't listening. No one is listening. And, anyway, it's a piece of information they all already know.

And Ruth, riding by the café on her bike, doesn't hear it either.
She's listening for something else: a tone, a skin tone, look-
ing to experience Kaliope with all her senses while noncha-
lantly pretending she doesn't notice the girl at all.
'I saw that chick in *NOW* magazine,' says Gustavo. 'She's a DJ.'
Kaliope takes a sip of her coffee. 'Really.'

There are stars in the sky that don't exist anymore.
Just because you see something doesn't mean it's there.

The City Is
always afraid of being a loser.
Who isn't?
When the winners are given so much, it's hard for anyone not
to feel a very deep terror at being anything but numero uno.
There are articles in the paper about a mathematician living
in that sexy city who discovered that any child could be a
math genius. Any single one of them. He claims that the
only thing standing between a little kid and mathematical
brilliance is supportive attention. If kids receive supportive
attention, they will be quickly ushered into the world of
beautiful numbers.
The same can be said about any ability.
All the city needs is a little loving attention. Its heat hovers
near forty degrees, breaking all records. The truth is: the
city's a hottie.
Still pimply, of course, but a wicked body.
A seed of self-confidence lies dormant and full of potential in
the belly of that place, the seed forming itself around the
certainty that the occupants are, themselves, sizzling, in
both senses of the word. They are a beautiful bunch.

Shy, though. Very shy.

They're like mice hugging the baseboards.

The person who figures out how to get those people out of their shells will become very rich. Or famous. Or both.

The key might be that everything wants to have sex, whether that's recognized or not. Maybe not sex, as such, but there's no doubt things want to smash together again and again and again.

There might be a key to the city hidden in that. Who knows.

I love you. I love you with all of my everything. So some say. Sometimes. Like when the day is hot, thick and covered with a blanket of humanity – no, *humidity*, we mean humidity.

Others say it's just the cicadas repeating *I love you, I love you, I love you,* automatically, like little metal robots designed by some military somewhere. Shhh. Listen to them.

The Day Is Sticky

in that sexy, pimply, beautiful, ugly, stupid, horny city. *I love yous* hover everywhere in the air, invisible but available to be grabbed, while cicadas buzz their languorous, electric song.

Up Yonge, the longest street in the solar system, past Highway 401, even further up past Highway 407, up tucked off to the side, is a long line of people, snaking their way around a jam-packed parking lot. In the middle of the line are Rani Vishnu and Michael Racco.

'Did you know,' says Rani, 'that the feet of a gecko stick to the wall because they become one with the wall at the atomic level?'

'Do you think they understand how the wall thinks?'
'They may feel how the wall feels.'

Blending is imperative; it's inevitable. Blending is being. The individual organs of your body only function because of their relationship to other organs.

The Vishnu Mandir

is a Hindu temple in Richmond Hill, a suburb of that sexy city. A long line of people stand waiting to experience the miracle, families a few generations wide from infants to great-great-grandmothers, all bringing milk to offer.

In the incredible heat of the afternoon, the black fleshy asphalt of the parking lot absorbs the rays of the sun and transmits them up and into the swelling and sweltering crowd.

'My feet feel like they're fusing with the ground,' says Rani as the throngs inch their way into the temple.

All the chairs in the main hall have been folded and leaned against the wall, while stanchions attached with red velvet ropes guide the devotees up and down the length of the room leading to a large porcelain statue of Lord Ganesh, looking happy to be there, entirely in the spotlight, the attention of the world at his pudgy feet.

Infants climb on parents and squirm and crawl all over the floors. One little kid makes his drooling way across the temple's carpets toward Michael and Rani. The child's mother steps forward and scoops the kid up.

'There seems to be an infiniteness about what I'm feeling,' says Rani.

'While still decidedly infinitesimal,' says Michael.

Another infant from another family crawls toward Rani and Michael.

'Occasionally, there's the sensation my skull has come open and a thickness denser than milkshake descends,' says Michael.

The line moves forward. Families talk quietly amongst themselves and infants occasionally cry. Two more small children break away from their families to crawl toward Rani and Michael, only to be intercepted by parents.

The statue's attendant signals Rani and Michael to step forward and hands them spoons in which dance a small quantity of milk. The kids lean toward the idol, clinking the spoon against the god's smooth tusks. The air in the temple becomes still, the tranquility interrupted only by the languorous buzzing of the occasional fat fly weaving through the devotees, hoping for a little milky offering itself.

Rani's spoon rests against one tusk and Michael's against the other.

And then the milk quickly vanishes, absorbed by the statue.

It's a miracle.

There's no doubt about it.

And it's happening all over the world.

Everywhere.

Some say it's a sign good times and prosperity are on the way, while others believe it prophesies the descent of a great soul to earth, coming down through the clouds to remove bondage and reveal righteousness.

Nothing is forever. That's the only thing you need to know.

Possessing the knowledge that nothing is forever will get you places you had no idea you could go. It's a passport to very specific dimensions. That, as some say, is good knowledge.

What Kind Of Knowledge

do you possess? That's a question being asked a lot. Who knows what and whose knowledge can be proven to be correct or incorrect have become almost all there is.

There's still kissing, though. Everybody knows about that. Kissing will probably never go away.

But what if kissing does go away? What if it just started to make no physical sense? What if it was definitively shown to simply serve a ritual function, like shaking hands or bowing? What if it drifted out of fashion?

Or what if an intense new sensitivity was forming? You wouldn't want to kiss anymore because the experience provided by the kiss could be better provided by sitting next to a person. The whole playing field would change. Sitting on a subway would become a whole other experience.

'I feel strange,' says little eleven-year-old Michael Racco to little eight-year-old Rani Vishnu as they sit together on the subway.

'Yes,' says Rani.

Is There A

revolution in confidence bubbling? Is that true? Can you feel it? Can we feel it?

It's hard to say. What if the first rule of the new confidence is that you can't refer to yourself as 'I' but, instead, 'we'?

Imagine doing that for a few hours. What do you think it would do to your head? Would it be a good thing or a bad thing? Think about it: we're all here anyway, why not just call things what they are? Is it creepy all alone inside your head? Try this: call out in the quiet of your mind. Call out: 'Hello!' Try it. Who's going to know? Who's going to care?

Go: 'Hello.'

Hello!

Did you hear that? That was us. We said hello back. Nice, isn't it? You're never alone.

Maybe you didn't hear it. Maybe you need to concentrate a little harder. Close the book, sit there and shout out 'Hello!' in the echoing emptiness of your own skull. And in the small silence that follows, you will hear something.

We promise.

And that sound, or word, or idea, or whatever, will be us, or something like us.

In any case, it's all the same thing.

Give it a whirl, listen carefully. We're not going anywhere. And, sadly, neither are you.

Close the book.

Okay, either you've done it or you haven't done it – there's no way around the simple truth of that. We've been formally introduced or we haven't. But why worry about formalities? Give us a kiss. Kiss the book – no one's watching. Just a peck would be fine; we've only just met.

And what if you felt our soft lips through the roughness of the page?

Kiss us. Now.

Down In The Darkness

of the Racco family basement, as the sun starts to set, Michael and Rani settle in with the television and a couple of grilled cheese sandwiches courtesy of Mrs. Racco.

Up Above And

through the ceiling, Katherine stands naked in her bedroom examining her belly in the mirror, tracing her hand down over her thickening nipples, down, circling her belly button, the radical changes to come only just noticeable.

Directly Below In

the family room, the television casts dancing light on dark wood-panelled walls; two plates, occupied only by the crusts of sandwiches, sit by themselves watching the news.
'Our members are not interested in any sort of compromise. If management thinks that, by leaving it in the lake, they can get rid of us, they're indulging in bad thinking. We will be with the tower whether it's up, down, floating in the lake or flying in the sky.'
The television keeps talking, the crusts of sandwiches continue watching, and off in a corner two small pairs of pants and a couple of T-shirts hang out beside a pile of sofa cushions fashioned into a small fort. If you poke through the tiny pile of clothing you won't find any socks. They're still being worn. But that's all that's being worn.
From the cracks in the sofa-cushion fort, heat emanates, the cool humidity of the basement gathering around and warming itself like Boy Scouts around a fire.

What's going on inside this sofa-cushion fort?

Do you want to know?

Should we let you inside?

The truth is, we can't. They're children, after all.

They could be up to any number of things.

Should we list the things? Would that be stating the obvious?
The truth is, we do want to get you in there. We want to tell
you what's happening; it doesn't seem like much to ask.

But we can't.

What we can do, though, is compile a list of the things that
could be going on, though it certainly wouldn't be a big
revelation. It might look like this:

Touching

Kissing

Sucking

Fucking

Pinching

Biting

Moaning

You get the picture. You probably already had the picture. But,
honestly, we're feeling a little excluded. If we had hands,
we'd rip apart the cushions and demand to see. We would
tell you every detail. There are simple joys occurring
beneath the cover of these cushions.

These are things, however, that you are forbidden to see –
forbidden, really, to even consider.

But, whatever, it's no big deal, it happens all the time. Go for
a walk around your neighbourhood, imagine you can see
through walls; there are kids messing around in almost
every basement. That's just what kids do.

A glow radiates from the cracks in the sofa-cushion fort. Or something like a glow.

Katherine Racco enters the room.

'It's awfully quiet down here.'

A man on the television says something about thundershowers. Katherine sits, reaches for the remote and shuts the TV off. She speaks to the small pile of cushions in the corner.

'You kids all right?'

'Yeah, Mom, we're fine.'

'Can I talk to you for a second?'

'I guess.'

'Michael ... Mommy's going to have a baby.'

Rani's voice emanates from the fort. 'Congratulations, Mrs. Racco.'

'Thank you, Rani. And you can call me Kathy.'

There's a small pause. The house is silent. In the distance there's the sound of a summer storm brewing as thunder rumbles.

'Do you understand, Michael? Mommy's going to have a baby.'

'What kind of baby?'

'Just a baby.'

'Where's Dad?'

'You know where Daddy is, honey. He's going to be there for a long time.'

The newest thing is a bubble-blowing solution that creates multicoloured sugary spheres which drift through the air as children chase and chomp them. Critics worry the particular polymer used to create the floating delicacies will clog the children's arteries. And it's true, a number of children have had heart attacks. But a definitive link can't be established, so the bubbles continue to sell.

Thirteen-Year-Old

James Hardcastle, back at the group home, is trying to fly from the top of one bunk to another when the doorbell rings. He opens the door to find little eleven-year-old Michael Racco.

'What's up?'

Michael doesn't say anything.

'Come in.'

Michael still doesn't say anything.

'You all right?'

'If you think you're going to be my stepdad, you can think again.

'I'm sorry?'

'Don't play dumb.'

'Hey, I don't have to play dumb.'

'If my mom doesn't have an abortion I'm going to knock her down the stairs and give her one.'

'I've never noticed how much you resemble your father.'

'Don't talk about my father.'

'Your father is my hero.'

'Yet you felt no remorse in banging his wife.'

'Who told you that?'

'I'm not stupid – I know how babies are made.'

'Look, kid, why don't you step inside and I'll whip up some Kool-Aid.'

'Why don't you step outside and I'll whip your ass.'

'Do you have a fever?'

'Listen, bastard – '

'Watch your mouth. I may not have had a dad but I'm no bastard. My old lady just started dividing the egg herself, everybody knows that.'

'Yeah, well, I wish I could say the same thing about my mom.'

'Well, Michael – '

'I can still smell her on you.'

'What are you talking about?'

'You know what I'm talking about.'

'All right, whatever, I sucked a little on her pussy while she was crashed out on Ativan but, really, if you know anything about biology you'll know all you get out of sucking pussy is a sweet taste in your mouth and a couple of pubic hairs in your throat. You certainly don't make a baby.'

'Look, pal, I said I know how babies are made.'

'From what I understand, she just starting dividing the egg herself, too, just like Joan. And she's probably going to have Children's Aid all over her ass, just like Joan.'

'What?'

'Hey, sport, everybody's doing it – it's a miracle!'

And maybe it's true. Maybe everybody is doing it. And if so, maybe it is a miracle. It certainly fits the description.

'Did you want the lime Kool-Aid or the cherry?'

A Little While

later, in the small covered courtyard at the back of the group home, the clink of ice adds a bit of music to the evening's conversation as the two boys enjoy the fresh flavour of lime.

'Money's money.'

'Who are these people?'

'They're just some people.'

'And what do you have to do?'

'Well, I've got to give them a demo reel first.'

'So you're just going to pose or something?'

'Well, you know, whatever.'

'Naked?'

'Naked? Of course, naked – this is money we're talking about!'

'And that's going to be enough to get you to Nunavut?'

'Well, it's a demo reel, and then I'll get work.'

Further West Along

College Street, walking up the tracks to the warehouse, Rani arrives home. She hears shouts of protest. She approaches the building in time to see a few guys hauling off the recently acquired appliances as cops guard. A piece of paper justifying the removal is offered. Citing concerns with health, zoning and fire hazards, the city insists it will bear responsibility for the feeding of the warehouse's residents. The residents are no longer permitted to cook for themselves.

All The Sewage

in that sexy city goes to the same place: the lake. Some of it is processed, sent through some kind of sieve, but during a rainstorm the system is overwhelmed; flood gates open and everything travels straight to the lake. It can be said that it's just a matter of priorities. But you can say that about everything. It's always all just a matter of priorities.

0

1

2

3

4

5

6

7

8

9

10

It's Morning And

a line of people snakes its way around the gravel parking lot of the warehouse, waiting to receive breakfast from the back of a truck. Young Rani takes her coffee, bowl of cold oatmeal and toast, soggy with margarine, and finds a place to sit near the railway tracks.

An older, curly-headed girl rolls up on an oversized tricycle. 'Give it to me.'

Rani hands over the cereal.

'And the coffee.'

Rani complies.

It's easy. She just lifts the cup, places it into the bigger girl's hand and lets it go. That's all it takes.

Is that a mantra from your life?

Just let it go. Let it all go.

Does that sound familiar?

Some people insist there are tiny speakers all over the world constantly whispering that very sentence into your ear, year after year.

Feeling healthy?

No?

Well, maybe that's why not.

Or, say you are feeling healthy. That's not so hard to achieve, is it? What's it take? A couple of laps around the block. Easy. Just let it all go.

A tall skinny white man with a large forehead stands in the dusty parking lot, flanked by two cops, and attempts to gather the attention of the residents of the warehouse.

He's ignored by most.

He explains that the residents of the warehouse are to be dispersed throughout the rest of the province and resettled in small cities and towns.

There will be a process of evaluation to match their skills with the needs of the various municipalities, with interviewers meeting residents throughout the week.

The small group has gotten bigger, and people begin to shout the man down, demanding the return of the stoves and fridges. The cops push back the crowd and the man retreats while handing out sheets of paper explaining the province's intentions. The flyers are tossed angrily into the air and scatter to the ground.

Rani sits on the periphery of a meeting where it's agreed that everyone will refuse the evaluation. A set of counter-demands is drafted: the appliances are to be returned and the warehouse is to be renovated into permanent apartments.

A commotion interrupts the meeting as members of the local business improvement association, teaming up with a disgruntled neighbourhood association, begin to picket the building. They are joined by a few carloads of strapping young white men just out of their teen years whose icy blue eyes appear to be eager for a scrap. The police, too, have gathered to restrain a counter-demonstration that begins to gather to protest the protesters.

Rani slips through the weeds, defying the moratorium on travel her mother has issued. Michael is standing on the tracks and together they take off as the sound of the clashing protesters wafts through the heavy summer air.

'What's The Difference

between moulding minds and melding minds?' Michael asks as they drift down the rails toward the chocolate factory. 'Aren't people usually attempting to mould others' minds in the image of their own – in effect, melding them?'

'I don't know,' Rani answers. 'Power knows that control is best exercised from a distance by ignoring rather than commanding, leaving you to control yourself. And if you somehow manage to get yourself not ignored, you'll end up in one of two scenarios: dumped by power, tossed out, murdered, jailed and so forth; or – if power can tax your gains – you will be promoted.'

'It's a dirty world,' says Michael.

'Melding minds, on the other hand, can only happen when the participants have more or less equal amounts of power, because the power is always shared,' continues Rani. 'Though equality has to be calculated as an average over the course of time.'

'Really?' says Michael.

'I think,' says Rani. 'I'm really just making all this up.'

'Really?'

'Though I seem able to make up these sorts of things only when I'm with you.'

'That's interesting.'

'It is. Mmmm. Can you smell the chocolate?'

Say you were a bar of chocolate. Wouldn't that be nice?

If you turn the lights off at night and gaze at yourself in the mirror, you might see your brain sparkling out from the roots of your hair.

Life is like light. So some say. Sometimes it's bright, sometimes it's dim. It can be reflected and distorted and you can never be sure of what you're seeing. It's important not to jump to any conclusions, not to start any rumours.

Rumours and innuendo are everywhere, all the time. In this city, in every city, in every town, in every village, in every home and in every head. All the time. It's a loud world. It's a noisy world.

It's a loud and noisy head on your shoulders.

What do you get when you cross loud and noisy?

It's a lousy world.

So some say.

It's A Hot

day. As hot as the breath between two kissing mouths on the cusp of coming. And as humid. Emergency cooling centres have been opened. The elderly, the young and those with respiratory difficulties are warned to stay inside; there's smog in the air. If you don't have AC, you can use a fan, the air flowing over you like warm blood. Clothing sticks and pulls on skin and asses are glued to pants, while air conditioners pump even more heat out on the streets. Some say the globe is warming at an alarming rate. Some say otherwise.

At her aunt's apartment, Kaliope spends time in bed thinking about all that existed before her and all that will exist after. Things are always bumping into each other. That much seems to be true and always.

Humans, so some say, are simply conductors carrying a message through time – a particular directive zipping faster than the speed of light, an idea that sometimes feels like a kid in a classroom, with her hand held high, being ignored by the teacher, an idea desperate for expression.

Last night, in the middle of the night, the telephone shattered Kaliope's sleep.

'I can hear you everywhere I go.' Ruth's voice, through the phone, was hot and wet like melted chocolate. 'I can hear the colour of your skin humming in my ears.'

Seventeen-Year-Old Grace Ng

knows there's no such thing as race, just degrees of distance from White, which casts its pale glow onto the world's populace, always landing, shading and shifting in intensity, casting you in light or in shadow.

Seventeen-year-old Gustavo Aguirre believes he's living his life with an eye toward the future – the present being such a mess. He feels his consciousness is perfectly suited to the kind of world that will erupt a few centuries down the road. As an emissary from the future, he knows that life in the present is, thus, always nothing but difficult.

Gustavo And Grace Stand

nervously in front of the door of Kaliope's aunt's apartment. Gustavo repeatedly presses the buzzer. They wait. Grace glances over her shoulder.

Kaliope opens the door.

'Hey.'

'We think we're being followed.'

Gustavo and Grace slip inside and climb the steep stairs.

'There are cop cars all over the place.'

'I've noticed.'

They enter the sweltering apartment.

'Where's the kid?' asks Gustavo, beads of sweat forming on his broad forehead.

'He's not here yet.'

Grace gravitates toward the massive bookshelf.

'Wow, that's a lot of books.'

'Yeah.'

Gustavo wipes his brow and lifts a video camera from his bag.

'Where are we going to do this?'

The doorbell rings.

'Here, anywhere, I don't care,' says Kaliope, leaving the room.

Gustavo focuses his camera on the books.

Grace pulls a book off the shelf, shuts her eyes and flips the pages randomly. She stops, selects a passage, opens her eyes and reads aloud.

'"More often, however, procedures of cultural genocide pioneered in North America seem to have become an item of export to countries sympathetic to such ideas of organization and development, bearing out Arendt's thesis on the commonality, even banality, of genocidal evil to a degree and in ways she – "'

James steps into the room, accompanied by Michael and Rani, followed by Kaliope, who does introductions.

'Thanks for this,' says James.

'I'll do what I can,' says Gustavo.

'Well, it's just a demo reel. It doesn't have to be too fancy.'

Gustavo Takes Responsibility

for the shoot, assigning the others various roles: Rani does James's makeup, evening the colour of the kid's skin, adding a few freckles and covering the dark circles under his eyes; Kaliope gathers lamps from all over the apartment and finds old pizza boxes to use as bounce boards; Michael heads to the kitchen and prepares craft services for the crew; while Grace documents the whole process with her Super 8 camera a few frames at a time, creating a fractured montage of the day's events.

James and Rani emerge from the bathroom. Gustavo approves of the makeup, assigns Rani the role of boom operator and positions James in front of a wall covered with a bright patterned cloth.

'We should get a real tight shot of your face to show the smoothness of your skin.'

'Whatever you say.'

'Okay, we're rolling! Quiet, please.'

Gustavo moves in closer with the camera. 'Okay, James, looking good. I need you to make your eyes just a little wider.'

James widens his eyes. James is a cute kid, there's little doubt about that – his body is on the cusp of its quantum leap into adulthood. His hair is a shiny silky tousle, getting a little long, his arms are almost elegant and lithe, and his bum, frankly, is not the kind usually associated with a boy of his age. A boy of any age. There is a strange and disconcerting curve to the kid's frame – alluring, maybe, depending on what you like to call home.

'Nice. Now if we could just have a smile so I can get a shot of your teeth.'

James complies.

'Very nice.'

'I floss every day.'

Gustavo steps back. 'Now, I think you should touch yourself a little.'

James' hand slides slowly up his abdomen to his chest.

'Slowly. Slowly. Nice. Now take off your shirt. Slow. Slow.'

The small T-shirt comes up over his head.

'Should I play with my nipples?'

'That could work.'

'I thought this was just a demo reel,' says Kaliope.

'It's fine,' says James. 'It's fine.'

The kid tweaks his nipples. They tighten, crinkling into small, hard pellets. He slowly trails his hand down past his belly button and into the front of his pants, his other hand coming up, the two thumbs hooking over the waist and sliding them off.

'Looking good,' says Gustavo.

Grace continues to squeeze off a few frames with her Super 8, focusing on the mesmerized production team.

James rubs himself through his underwear. The temperature in the room rises, the air becomes dense.

James inches his underwear down, keeping his gaze glued to the camera's lens. He pulls the briefs over his slightly generous bum to reveal his glistening genitals.

'What the – ?'

Gustavo stops shooting.

'What?'

'Where are your balls?'

'I don't have balls.'

'*What?*

'I don't have balls.'

'What have you got?'

'Whatever, dude, I got what I got.'

'Let me look at that thing. What is this? He's got a dick and a pussy?'

Everybody crowds around James.

Michael steps into the room with a bowl of jujubes.

'What's the commotion?'

'The guy's got a pussy!'

'What?'

'What difference does it make?'

'Well, I don't know, I thought there might be some marketing concerns.'

'Whatever, *Boys with Pussies*. I don't care, that's not my problem.'

'I guess.'

'Roll the camera, guy.'

'This could make you a lot of money,' says Rani.

'Now we're talking.'

The heat of the apartment spikes as the video crew becomes silent, all more or less mesmerized by young James's newly revealed attributes. The air is oppressive, sweat trickling down foreheads, necks, the quiet occasionally broken by the brief whirring of Grace's Super 8 camera. A fat fly cruises around the room as Rani inches the boom closer, capturing James's increasingly laboured breathing as the kid begins to play with himself.

'Okay,' Gustavo croaks, a bead of sweat rolling down his face.

James's arm begins to pick up speed, becoming a blur. His eyes drift shut, his mouth opens and his consciousness loses touch with the room, retracting fully into his young body, forgetting the trivialities of time and space. He begins to make sounds and move his hips around, fingers slick and slippery. His pelvis jerks back and forth, twitching and tensing while spasms rattle the whole scene. His breathing becomes deeper and tight little grunts escape from his throat, gradually rising in pitch. And then the kid falls backward, landing on the futon, cresting the cusp of coming. There's the standard shaking and jerking and moaning, which gives way to laughter.

'What's so funny?'

James's laughter subsides. The kid sits there on the mattress, eyes bright, a sheen of sweat glazing his young naked body.

'Whew,' says the kid. 'That was all right.'

While Tidying Up

the apartment, Grace speaks to Kaliope. 'You're very photogenic.'

'Thanks.'

James lifts the cassette and smiles. 'Wish me luck.'

'Be careful.'

Then the little boy is down the stairs and out the door.

Nobody Cares About

the things in the back of your head that you've hidden from everybody. Secrets.

Or maybe they do.

Have you ever chopped someone into little pieces? Of course you have. Who hasn't?

Even if it was just yourself.

A few things: assume everything you think you know is propaganda, learn fast, forget faster, know this place was created in agony and can only disappear in agony, and your pain is a product like everything else.

Or maybe you're not in pain. It doesn't matter; the same applies to your pleasure.

0

1

2

3

4

5

6

7

8

9

10

The City Has

ground to a halt. Whistles are blowing and the Super City Summer Festival, spanning the last week in July and the first week in August, is happening everywhere. Events of all sorts swirl in the streets: cultural, spiritual, sexual and sporty; there's pageantry, picnics and dense crowds of beautiful scorching people jostling to board the ferries to the Toronto Islands. Some streets are closed, temporary tents erected all over the place, street vendors and restaurants cooking animals outside on barbecues, the mouth-watering odour mixing with the heavy clouds of car exhaust trapped by the thick hot blanket of humidity.

The Super City Summer Festival is happening during the hottest part of the year, each year hotter. Ever more water hangs in the air – water formerly locked in ice here and there but now released and, with nowhere else to go, just hanging out in the atmosphere watching the summer as it unfolds.

The humidity is laid back. It has no worries. It spends the summer downtown with the car exhaust, enjoying the beautiful weather.

The humidity loves itself but has little concern for you. It wants you to like it, but if you don't it's no big deal. The humidity knows not to take things personally – a fundamental step in the quest for enlightenment, and the humidity is well on its way.

People complain about the humidity. But people complain about everything.

Concerts big and small are happening all over the city, indoors and outdoors, daytime and night. Products flow to consumers in a never-ending stream of promotions: sunscreen, soft drinks, gum, hair product. Children are lost in crowds, some never to return.

At the very height of the Super City Summer Festival, on the Saturday of the long weekend in August, there's a massive celebration organized by the city's Caribbean community. It features dances, parties, shopping, eating and, the event's highlight, a parade filled with mas bands, huge costumes on wheels, steel drums and lots of winin'.

The newspapers love to feature accounts of problems among the organizers, but business is addicted as tourists pour in from all over the globe, making it the continent's biggest gathering, a parade bigger than the one Santa Claus throws. People dance in the sunshine, packed tight along Lakeshore Boulevard, the chime of the steel drums mixing with the smell of the hot dogs, the crowd bouncing and bouncing, blowing whistles and lifting their arms in the air, the sun grinning at them.

Kaliope Vally And

Grace Ng move through the parade, Gustavo trailing, keeping an eye out.

'You know,' Grace says to Kaliope, 'there's something about your radiance that speaks of fame.'

'I have no idea what you're talking about.'

'I wonder if that spirit can be caught by a camera.'

'You're welcome to try.'

'I think we're being followed,' says Gustavo.

Gustavo feels that he was born to be followed.

He always maintains that, considering the current state of the world, it's important to be the kind of person the authorities keep their eye on, though sometimes that can prove to be only too easy.

But during times like these, if you can't get yourself spied on, then what good are you? Gustavo hopes any actions he takes will be enough of a threat to be of interest to the state. And there certainly are strange clicks on his phone – but there are strange clicks on everybody's phone. Perhaps you, yourself, are a strange click.

'Teeth are brilliantly designed.' The din of the steel drums forces Kaliope to shout as she shows her teeth for the benefit of Grace's camera. 'Having a mouth full of bits of bone that spend our whole lives threatening to rot and fall out grounds the understanding of decay right inside our faces. We're constantly kicked with the realization that death, in the end, will be the last word to tumble out of our mouths.'

There's a camera on you, too. Always. There's always the possibility your actions will be reproduced elsewhere. Even if just by yourself, as you do the same things over and over again. You are a camera watching you, recording you, reproducing you.

So some say.

Over Here, Ruth Racco

scans the crowd, her ears like parabolic dishes, gathering signals that are bouncing everywhere, searching for the tone generated by Kaliope's skin. She finds the air filled with the harmonics of the city's many shades.

She tries to connect what she hears with what she feels, hoping that when she locks on to to Kaliope's frequency she'll be able to sink the sensation into her heart and never let it go, binding the two for eternity.

Ruth starts to feel the heat and begins to move with the crowd, her body constricted by her clothes – a baseball cap, long sleeves and pants reaching down to her feet – and sunscreen covering her hands. She has only ever danced in the darkness of clubs, or in the shade of her bedroom or at the brightly lit wedding receptions of cousins. She has never danced in the sunshine.

Ruth believes adulthood begins with the awareness of dance as a form of communication, as a way to relate to others, a form of seduction.

Were genitals always a part of dancing? Ruth couldn't remember but she doesn't think so, at least not consciously. It was the self-consciousness of dancing that signified a transitory period from the child to the adult. And that could happen at any time. The child becomes the adult gradually, aspect by aspect.

The child creates, the teenager becomes aware of the power of creation and the adult chooses which direction to point that power, through a manoeuvre that sees the individual giving way to the power of creation itself.

Ruth wants to be dancing in the sunshine.

The sun is alive, there is little doubt about that. Or so some say. Others say the sun is life itself. And there's little doubt about that, either.

The tree is simply an extension of the sun, an expression of the sun on earth, as is the fruit that grows on the trees and the animals that eat it. This is a teenage discovery. An adult tries to figure out which plants to eat to get certain things happening.

All around Ruth there are people jumping up and down, steel drums chiming and whistles screaming.

The Sound Of

calypso travels through the air above the train tracks, just managing to reach the roof of the warehouse. Little eleven-year-old Michael Racco and little eight-year-old Rani Vishnu talk within the lush green of the garden, tangled in the pumpkin vines. The hot sun sizzles their bodies and ultraviolet rays pierce their skin, stimulating melanocytes into activity.

Some say melanin is a little-understood substance, capable of superconductivity, able to absorb light and sound – it's said to be the body's connection to the world. A miraculous substance.

'I think, by definition, a miracle defies rational explanation,' says Rani.

'But many unexplained things have eventually been understood.'

'Well, that's what I'm talking about. The things we think are miracles are just the things yet to be explained.'

'Then life is full of miracles.'

'Keeping the populace reaching for a beauty already right in front of them, while at the same time denying the very existence of this grace, is one of this civilization's most effective tools for controlling the imagination.'

The sound of the neighbourhood association's picket wafts up on the humid air.

Michael reaches out and touches Rani's head. 'You've got another grey hair.'

Rani and Michael close their eyes to the sun. Strands of protein float in the fluid between the lids and the corneas, sometimes almost forming words.

Some say the written word is based on these swirls.

The breathing of the two children slows in the relaxed heat, their eyes drifting up and flickering, vibrating, muscles occasionally twitching in short bursts of energy.

Calypso Is Screaming

out of the speakers and people are jumping up, the crowd pouring onto the street.

Grace focuses the camera on Kaliope as she presses the sky upward, keeping it from falling. Beads of sweat jump off Kaliope's forehead. Grace speeds up the camera, spreading light across more frames, slowing down the action.

Kaliope is in the centre of her world, no concerns dragging her anywhere, all of her attention hovering no more than a couple of centimetres above her skin.

Kaliope dances toward Grace's camera while Grace clicks off frame after frame, the film happy to allow the girl's image to scorch its emulsion.

The Body Is

an antenna and fun is being broadcast across the universe. If you're lucky, the fun can take you in its arms and give you the biggest and warmest of hugs. A hug as big and warm as that of the sun. The sun loves you. You were born and you live of its energy. Haven't you noticed? Look at yourself, you're hot.

Folding herself into the parade, Ruth removes her hat and tosses it into the air, her white curly hair spilling out, and dances hard with the crowd. She removes her shirt, ties it to her waist and dances in her bra, letting the sun grace her body fully.

She drinks in the rays, consumes them, inhales them and absorbs them, incorporating the sun's energy into her movements. Her dance is a frenzy, her white hair flashing out from her head, her white skin blinding in intensity. She shucks off her pants and lets them fall behind. Her costume is a little plain: ordinary underwear and a sports bra.

Ruth feels that she is everything and, as such, is always united with Kaliope.

When's the last time you felt one with everything? It doesn't happen every day, if it happens at all.

And maybe it shouldn't.

It's not a very pleasant sensation.

While Over Here,

quick, there's seventeen-year-old Gustavo Aguirre, his arms pinned behind his back by two large white men. They hold his wrists and elbows and lead him quietly away from the parade. He struggles, but their grip is unrelenting; they know the special places to hold to make bodies comply.

If you were to float high in the sky above the parade, you would see similar events all over as small snatch squads scour the route, little photocopied booklets in white men's hands with stills from surveillance videos. People are being picked up for any number of misdemeanours: skipped meetings with immigration officials, failure to register a change of address, unpaid phone bill. An entire community gathered, scoured – individuals plucked like dark fruit.

Back On The Roof,

Rani and Michael breathe, their gently rising solar plexuses lifting belly buttons up into the sky, past lacy clouds, past planets, past stars, to the outer reaches of the universe, bumping against the very curve of space.

Then an exhale, their diaphragms pushing inward, travelling to tiny infinities, stretching inward, inching lower, deeper, further, until only two molecules of oxygen are left in the lungs, then one, then none.

An emptiness suddenly appears in the stomachs of the two kids, a sink hole, like the plug has been pulled on a basin of thick warm mud, the bottom suddenly dropping out, the two kids dropping through the hole to find themselves in a place of no time, frozen somewhere near the apex of a roller coaster waiting to plunge, the sensation of everyone here being right there.

'Hey,' the children say.

Hey, we say back.

And Over Here, Ruth,

with her eyes wide, seeing the sound of it all – the yellow and green of the steel drums, the purple bass, blue whistles – is hit with a tsunami of nausea. She staggers out of the parade, pushing through the crowd, out onto the empty open grass near the lake, her jaws apart, her diaphragm contracting, as she vomits.

And as she vomits, something detaches from her body. Or her body detaches from something.

What if you were pulled inside out? And kept alive? All of your sense organs, now turned in on themselves, able to connect only with each other – your mouth speaking only to your ears, your ears hearing only your voice, and your eyes able to look only at the back of your head.

Your internal organs would be left hanging in the sunshine, themselves, left alone to interact with the world. They would have to invent new languages to get along, new gestures – gestures better suited to the nuances of smooth muscle, muscles controlled by the autonomic nervous system, a system that does whatever it wants. You would be simply along for the ride.

But it's not like you would have nothing to do, don't worry about that. Feeling is doing. That's an important aspect of life on earth. Feeling is most definitely doing.

If you're just standing around and someone asks what's up, you can always talk about your feelings like they are accomplishments.

In an ideal world, anyway. That world exists. There is a place that's good. Just good. A place that's strictly goodness. You've been there. Maybe you're there now. How's the weather?

And then –

And Then There's

a rapid succession of gunshots, screams. The crowd fragments, everybody sprints for safety in different directions.
People slam into other people in blind desperation. Grace
drops her knee to the ground, holds the camera steady and
keeps shooting, following Kaliope who catches the wave of
panic and whirls around, twisting like a piece of DNA in the
breeze as people bolt in every direction possible.

Things Stretch.

And Then The

two from the roof of the warehouse, Rani and Michael,
suddenly break in, then Ruth joins us, and here's Kaliope.
'What's happening?' they all say.

Not too much, we say.

'Things seem to have come to a complete stop,' Kaliope points
out.

It's been like this for ages, we say.

'What do you do for fun?' asks Ruth.

Just this, we say.

'Just this?' Rani asks. 'Just this sensation of being at the apex
of a rollercoaster?'

That's about it, we say.

'I guess it's never boring,' Michael says.

It's tough to beat a nice even mix of sheer terror and pure joy,
we say.

'I guess if you've got that going on,' Kaliope says, 'you should
consider yourself fortunate.'

Well, that's what we tell ourselves, we say.

'There's the feeling of intense affection. Love, even,' Rani
observes.

Yes, we say, we're not sure what that is.

'And sadness,' Ruth adds.

Yeah, it can be rough, we say.

'There's the desire to blend and blur,' Kaliope says.

Yes, that feeling happens to everyone.

'May we?' they all ask.

We don't see why not, we say.

They begin to blend and blur, merging with us. All of us. With you.

You. You sitting there with this book in your hands.

Can you feel them? Look carefully, scan your body for traces. Rani, Michael, Kaliope and Ruth are trying to enter you – us. And, believe it or not, they're succeeding.

Stop reading. Stare off into space. Listen for them. Look for them. Feel for them.

And then the kids inhale. And are gone. Back on the roof. Back in the parade, remembering nothing of our conversation.

Kaliope Remains Calm

in the centre of the maelstrom: it becomes an altar upon which she can offer a prayer to her relevance.

Gunshots bouncing around a packed parade is the kind of thing people write books about, make movies about; a shooting in the middle of the biggest gathering on the continent is something that makes the news.

If you're there when it happens, then you are the news. You are where the action is at.

This is something you will whisper to others in the dead of a hot and sticky night, certain you have endured the most important event of the day, of the week, certainly of the moment.

'I saw someone get shot today.' Your voice will be hushed, the clinking of ice cooling your warm drink, your body filled with the incident, horrified but amplified, distilling the event down into something that can silence a room full of people and bring everything to bear on yourself.

'Really?' the room full of people will ask.

'Really,' you will say and you will describe how time slowed and chaos reigned.

Kaliope stands in the middle of the chaos, completely aware of Grace's camera and, with the sound of the gunshots still reverberating in the air, feels like her life matters. This is, in itself, a confusing thing to feel as a bullet flies through the air looking for a life to shatter.

A woman is downed, caught in some kind of crossfire between young men trying to settle scores. Or, at least that's what the news will report.

People are yelling, screaming, running. Kaliope stares stunned into Grace's camera as she feels her feet leave the ground, her confusion turning to horror. There are more shouts as people begin to notice Kaliope drifting upward as Grace continues documenting.

The crowd can't decide what's more pressing, the woman felled and bleeding or the teenager floating in the air. People scream.

And On The

roof: shouts shatter the stillness of the air. People pour out onto the rooftop, riot cops protecting city workers in overalls carrying shovels and industrial-strength garbage bags who begin tearing up the garden. There are shouts of protest and the grunts of warehouse inhabitants being beaten by cops and screams of anger. Dirt flies everywhere, tomatoes just beginning to blush are crushed, roots are ripped, dirt still clinging, and shoved into garbage bags. Rani and Michael are scooped by a shovel and tossed into the air.

'My baby!' Anu shouts. Cops restrain her. Others are pinned to the ground, knees on spines. The two children scream and tumble in the dirt, tumble between the legs of the men dismantling the garden, tumble between the legs of the cops who reach out and grab, the kids squirting like soap between their fingers, bouncing around the roof. People are shoved hard, the chaos spreading all over the roof like a pool of blood.

Rani is knocked by a cop's shield, out and over the roof's edge, tumbling into space.

Anu screams. 'My baby!'

Rani's eyes are wide as she goes over.
Michael reaches out to her.
And misses.

Rani seems to hover for a second, like a coyote in a cartoon.
Then she begins to rise, her eyes growing even wider.
Michael leaps off the roof.
He, too, rises, both kids floating up and eastward toward the city's centre, toward all the glittering buildings.
'Rani!' Anu screams.

A cop pulls out a gun and empties it at the floating children. The bullets whiz past as the kids rapidly become mere dots in the sky.

Are You Looking

for different dimensions? Well, they're here, right now. They're everywhere, in fact.

You can think of mood as a place, if you want, a place you can visit occasionally, frequently, or a place, in fact, where you can live.

This dimension of mood as place is founded on the quantification of quality, the dividing up of feeling sets. You can travel between them since they are, literally, different places. Things encountered as outside your body are the mechanical functions of your vehicle, and they affect the journey's progress just like a broken fan belt, dirty spark plugs or shaky transmission does.

You are everything that is here, now, making itself known through your flesh as a particular mood-place which your flesh and, in turn, everything else inhabits.

The best way to get from one mood-place to another is by pointing yourself in the direction you want to go and hitching a ride on what is happening now. But remember that now is alive and living with you, like a voice in your head. And now can talk. Listen to it. If you like.

'Okay, I will,' thinks Ruth, as she becomes lost in an ocean of unconsciousness, moorings abandoned, her body lying over here, down by the lake, stricken, comatose and sizzling in the day's blazing sun. The 'Okay, I will' being the last thing to wilfully cross her mind.

With A Bump,

Rani and Michael come to rest among the trees on Ward's Island, one of the Toronto Islands, not too far from the structure formerly known as the world's tallest.

The islands are simply some sandbars that have been home to, among other things, Babe Ruth's first professional home run. And, before that, for thousands of years, a place for people to hang out. The islands float at the bottom of the city, south of the glistening buildings and across the harbour. Preferring the view of the lake, they keep their backs to the metropolis.

Rani and Michael walk south toward the beach, traversing a marsh thick with vegetation. The summer is at its absolute apex. Tadpoles shoot around the kids' feet, thick meaty creatures just on the verge of bursting into frogs.

The two kids reach into the warm still water and lift handfuls of the little animals, feeling them tickle against their palms, trying to wiggle through cracks between fingers. They release them, watching them dart for cover.

Michael spots a large one, stuck and struggling in a tight tangle of dark and decaying weeds, its new legs trying to push for freedom. Rani reaches down to emancipate the creature, lifting it and holding it in her open palm. The tadpole at first appears like a new kind of animal with something different about its structure, additional limbs hanging off its side. The two kids focus, trying to decode the strange image.

The realization they are looking at two creatures causes the kids to jump: a large metallic insect has clamped its jaws clamped around the fat juicy body of a tadpole that's thrashing in a futile attempt at escape.

Rani tosses the two creatures back into the swamp. Michael grabs her hand and the two wade quickly through the weeds and warm water and out of the marsh to ascend a sand dune.

The beach stretches in front of them, the pale sand hot on their feet as they cross, peel off their clothing and plunge into the soothing waters.

The lake is clean. As clean as anything can get these days. There's a little bacteria here and there, but the same holds true for your mouth.

They float on their backs, staring up at a blue sky streaked with thin strands of the occasional cloud, the water as warm as amniotic fluid.

The sun begins its descent and the darkness begins to rise, the sound of water the only thing in the kids' ears.

Blackness leaks into the sky, muted by the glare from the city, but still strong enough to offer an elegant backdrop for a light smattering of stars.

A meteor streaks the sky.

Then another. And another. Every minute a new star falls – the sky alive with the blazing deaths of celestial fragments, some as small as a grain of sand, the largest as big as a pebble. Hundreds fall over the course of the night. At each instance, the two children wordlessly make the same wish over and over again, as their bodies are buoyed by the calm waters, calm enough to eventually induce a floating slumber.

That Night Someone

has a dream. In the dream there is a beautiful beach, beautiful clean water. There are people standing on the hot sand. They're looking to the sky and crying to the heavens to send help. They send beams of light into space from the centre of their foreheads, a radiant sos

The dreamer feels fine, nestled in a small swamp among the trees, staring up through the surface of the water, the light bending and presenting the distorted image of desperate humans seeking rescue. Then, suddenly, there is pain as the dreamer dreams of being bitten. Then struggle is all there is. Through and through.

A secret: this moment, this moment here, is your central command. You are sitting at central command. Is this what you expected it to look like? Are you unsure of how to behave here? Don't worry, it's easy. All you have to do is assess the situation accurately, act accordingly, share and be good. So some say. Some things should be easy and this moment is one of them. It's easy: you're reading a book. What more needs to be said?

We could say more: let's say, as you sit there reading this book, there are bugs crawling all over your body. Can you feel them? They're crawling on your legs, tickling you slightly, a small wiggling between your clothing and your skin. They're on your torso, your belly, in the curve of your back, your chest, between your shoulder blades, on your neck and all over your face, your eyes, your nose and especially your mouth.

It's true, you are covered with bugs. There are microscopic bugs crawling all over you, all the time. They eat you as you die. That's their job, their destiny.

And yours is to die. What could be more simple?

The Sun Cracks

the cloudless horizon, lifting itself sluggishly, peeking westward through the gaps between the glittering buildings, the heat already oppressive, the partying city resting now, nursing a hangover, streets still covered in scattered detritus: dirty hot dogs, paper plates, flyers and streamers. Portable toilets sit, quiet with indigestion, while bleachers, folded up and stacked, wait to be stored until the next big event. Small clumps of people wander aimlessly, looking wired and tired, still amplified by the previous night's activities, looking for a coffee or something to calm it all down.

At The Warehouse

there's smoldering chaos as the authorities restore an order which, for most of the night, has been lost. Large parts of the building have been torched – by the occupants, so the newspapers claim.

There's some debate about that.

School buses have been ordered to the scene; some sit idling in the dusty parking lot near the building, while some have already departed, taking people and dispersing them around the province, atomizing the group, sending them to a variety of communities, mostly rural areas experiencing a shortage of farm labour.

Rani and Michael move through the weeds of the rail lines. Rani picks up speed, running, Michael following close behind.

'Rani!' Anu lifts the child, hugging her tight.

A paramedic approaches. 'Is she okay?'

A cop calls out. 'We need everybody over here.'

'What's your name?' the paramedic asks.

'Rani.'

'That's a pretty name.'

'Over here!' shouts the cop. Anu moves toward one of the buses, Rani still in her arms. Michael follows. Rani looks back at him over Anu's shoulder.

'Bye,' says Michael.

Rani lifts her espresso-bean necklace over her head and holds it out to Michael. He reaches for it.

A cop, high on a horse, calls down. 'Get out of here.'

The necklace drops to the ground. The cop angles his horse, Michael having to duck down to reach quickly between the horse's legs to pick up the necklace before being forced toward the crowd of onlookers who have gathered on the street.

The bus pulls out of the parking lot. Rani gazes out through a dirty window and locks eyes with Michael. The two kids stare at each other, the rest of the world becoming misty, inchoate, barely there.

The bus pulls out onto the street. Michael fades into the distance. The bus is gone.

0

1

2

3

4

5

6

7

8

9

10

The Sky Is

dark, the first cold rain of September deciding whether or not to fall.

Michael sits reading the newspaper beside Ruth's hospital bed as she lies in a coma, various machinery sustaining her with tubes entering via holes punctured in her arms and throat, her entire body wrapped in clean bright gauze, she, now, whiter than ever.

Michael wears a mask, protecting him from the pneumonia keeping his sister teetering on the edge of death.

His eye is caught by a headline in the newspaper he holds: 'Waterwalker Uncovers Ice.' It features a photograph of James Hardcastle. The article explains that the boy has recently unearthed a bunch of diamonds in Nunavut. The kid's freckled face beams out from a large colour photograph. 'I've never been interested in diamonds, I was just digging for a friend,' the quote reads. Michael follows the article into the paper and comes across a photo of Kaliope, hovering a few inches off the ground, signing autographs during a stop in Iqaluit, Nunavut, on the Arctic leg of her national tour. The headline reads: 'Flying Teen Visits Arctic.'

Katherine enters the room, her stomach bulging with the new addition to the family. She sits beside Michael and glances at her comatose daughter.

Michael Stands In

the hospital pharmacy staring at a rack of snacks. He lifts a package of peanuts and examines them. He's never spent much time looking at peanuts. He's surprised to see they are so oily. Why would people eat these little greasy pellets? He walks to the counter and lays down a few coins.

Michael Walks Through

Kensington Market as rain begins to spit, holding his package of peanuts a little away from his body.

'Hey.'

Michael looks up to see Grace.

'What's up?' she asks.

'Not much.'

'How's Ruth?'

'The same.'

Grace nods.

'Any word on Gustavo?' Michael asks.

'Still holding him, no charges.'

'How are you?' asks Michael.

'I'm taking off for a bit.'

'Yeah?'

'*The Flight of Kali* is screening in a few places.'

'Where?'

'You know, Berlin, Brussels and a festival in Italy.'

'Nice.' Michael lifts his hand. 'You want a peanut?'

'No, I'm okay. I should go.'

'See you.'

'Later.'

Say You Can

fly.

Just say it: 'I can fly.'

What might that be like?

Let's say it's like this: it's just a matter of thinking particular
thoughts.

That's it. That's the mechanism.

It's something about your relation to the rest of the world. It's about forgetting the many things you've always been told to remember. It's about blending and blurring and believing, finally, that you're no longer there, but instead every-where – everybody with you, somehow cheering you on. Whether everybody knows they're cheering you on or not.

Maybe. Or maybe not.

Maybe you'll never be able to fly no matter what you think of yourself and everybody else. Or maybe you're the kind of person who is always hovering a bit in the air. Maybe you have to siphon off the energy of others to do so. Who's going to notice? Most people will always blame themselves first for any fatigue they feel. In any case, let's just say you can fly. Say it:

I can fly.

Now do it. Fly.
Fly.
Just give it a try. Fly.

Or, at least imagine you can – that being the first step toward getting anything done.

Imagine you're doing it now. You're rising over Bellevue Park as little eleven-year-old Michael Racco sits beneath a tree and opens his bag of peanuts. You rise higher and are able to see Dundas Street to the south, the Alexandra Park proj-ects and, to the west, the Alexandra Pool, to the east, Spadina Avenue and Chinatown. You rise higher, able now to see the Happy Bean, then College Street, Harbord Street, Bathurst and beyond to Euclid and the house Ruth and Kaliope shared. Then the city is just a mass of colour and, as you enter the dark clouds, the place disappears, a fork of lightning blasts a 'hello' in your direction as you pass by, upward, beyond the clouds, through the atmosphere, to where there is no air, to where there is nothing but inky blue, you and a few stars pushing their way through the dying day. Flying higher and higher, the blackness consuming you as the vacuum of space starts to pull, jealous that you're so damn together.

And in response, you begin to unravel, your D N A unwinding and splitting apart, exploding into the night, the warm blue planet below you: a happy tiny smiling ball. Your pieces pull fully apart as your flight reaches the end of its momentum.

You pause now, your atomized fragments floating for a moment, uncertain what to do next, hovering between here and there, just a slight beat before the rush of the planet's gravity beckons you back.

'Come on,' the earth says. 'It wasn't so bad, was it?'

Was it?

No, it wasn't, was it?

Was it?

Your atoms, unable to resist the globe's charm, begin to fall, gaining speed as they approach the earth, piecing themselves together, entering the atmosphere in a great fiery ball, as you reconstitute, flaming through the air, gathering rain as you punch through the clouds and rocket toward the ground, you, a torrential downpour dumping on the sad and lonely occupants of that stupid and confused city.

And let's say you land, right where you began, standing in the middle of the park. The rain hammers down on you, soaking you. You shiver. Across from you sits Michael, under a tree, catching some cover from the deluge. He looks at the peanuts in the package. He pours them into his palm. He smells them.

The rain continues to pour. You pull your jacket tight around your body, trying to scrape up some warmth.

You watch Michael lift Rani's necklace over his head, open the small metal container, pour out the coffee beans and fill it with a few peanuts. He closes it, lifts it over his head and tucks it under his shirt. He stands and walks away from the tree, out and into the rain, tossing the remainder of the peanuts onto the wet ground.

The rain cascades.

Your cellphone rings.

You reach into your pocket and pull it out.

'Hello?' you say.

'Hey,' says the voice of young James Hardcastle. 'I'm here in Nunavut with Kaliope.'

'Oh, yeah?' you say.

'Yeah. We just called to say hi.'

You hear Kaliope in the background: 'Hi.'

So you say, 'Hi.'

'Hi,' says James.

Then you hear Kaliope. 'Okay, now, say goodbye, my agent's supposed to call.'

'I've got to go,' says James. 'Later.'

And then the phone goes dead.

Dead.

Sense your death. You can do it. It is possible.

Go on.

For just a second.

What can it hurt?

Don't think about it, sense it.

You just have to say to yourself, 'Go,' and in the moment before a single thought can appear you will feel something small and something fast and that will be your death's contours: the date, location, cause and weather. You will be able to sense it all. But you'll have to be attentive – it's a tiny moment.

What's it hurt to try, right? Why not? Give it a whirl.

You might want to be lying down – it can be a shock.

Comfortable?

Okay. On three.

One ...

Two ...

Oh, wait, but first there's this: let's just say that, after that death, you will be the baby that's now floating in Katherine's uterus.

Because you will, you really will.

Okay ... and ...

Three.

Thanks To

Alana Wilcox for guidance throughout the process.

And thanks – for a variety of reasons – to: Carmen Aguirre, Kirsten Azan, John Barbeito, Oliver Barnett, Hamani Bannerji, Rose Bellosillo, Stan Bevington, Adrian Blackwell, Laura Blaise, Tyler Clark Burke, Naomi Campbell, Sarah Chase, Yen Chu, John de Jesus, Nicky Drumbolis, David Findlay, Tony Glenesk, Karen Hanson, Mike Hoolboom, Rochelle Hum, Instant Coffee, Rosina Kazi, Min Sook Lee, PJ Lilley, Michelle Lowry, Jay MillAr, Jason McBride, John Mighton, Nick Murray, Yvonne Ng, the Ontario Coalition Against Poverty, Christina Palassio, Rebecca Picherack, Marco Racco, Rick/Simon, Jeff Shantz, Tanisha Sri Bhaggiyaddatta, Kika Thorne, Shiraz Vally, Sean Vishnu, Darren Wershler-Henry, Saoirse Shantz, Dan Young, Libby Zelek.

The Epigraph

is from 'Means without ends: notes on politics' by Giorgio Agamben (reprinted in *Cities Without Citizens*, edited by Eduardo Cadava and Aaron Levy.

The lyrics on page 134 are from Stylistics' 'Stone in Love with You' by Bell, Creed and Bell.

The quote on page 176 is from *Since Predator Came* by Ward Churchill.

Darren O'Donnell Is

a writer, director, designer, performance artist and artistic director of Mammalian Diving Reflex. His performances include *A Suicide-Site Guide to the City*, *pppeeeaaaccceee*, *White Mice*, *[boxhead]*, *Who Shot Jacques Lacan?*, *Radio Rooster Says That's Bad* and *Over*. He was the 2000 recipient of the Pauline MacGibbon Award for directors and has been nominated for a number of Dora Awards for his writing, directing and acting and has won for design. He also received a 2000 Gabriel for excellence in broadcasting. Darren organizes the *Talking Creature*, an ongoing social experiment on the art of conversing with strangers. Coach House Books has published *Inoculations: Four Plays* (2001) and *pppeeeaaaccceee* (2003). This is his first novel.

Typeset in Scala and printed and bound at the Coach House on
bpNichol Lane, 2004

Edited and designed by Alana Wilcox
Author photo by Troy O'Donnell
Cover design by Rick/Simon
Cover art by Tyler Clark Burke, courtesy of the artist

Coach House Books
401 Huron Street (rear) on bpNichol Lane
Toronto, Ontario
M5S 2G5

416 979 2217
1 800 367 6360

mail@chbooks.com
www.chbooks.com